KNO

BLOODBATH

ORDER OF THE UNSEEN

INTERNATIONAL BESTSELLING AUTHOR
MOLLY DOYLE

All rights reserved.
Copyright © 2024 by Molly Doyle

This book is a work of fiction. Any names, characters, places, and events are products of the author's imagination, and any resemblance to actual events or places or persons, living or dead, is entirely coincidental.

Edited by The Havoc Archives
Blurb by Author BL Mute
Cover Design by DesignsbyCharlyy
Formatting by DesignsbyCharlyy

CONTENT WARNINGS

This is a Dark Romance/Suspense, Why Choose. Bloodbath contains mature and graphic content that is not suitable for all audiences. Content warnings include aftercare, anal, barebacking, begging, bipolar disorder, blood, blood play, breath play, cult, death, dismemberment, dissociation, fingering, gore, group sex, human sacrifice, intrusive thoughts, knife play, marking, mental distress, murder, mutilation, oral, praise, rough sex, stalking, substance use, torture, violence.

AUTHORS NOTE

The content within this book is FICTIONAL and NOT to be used as a guide for anything related to real life. Please DO NOT grind your pussy on the knife that is covered with the blood of the men your boyfriend slaughtered, etc

Be smart.
Be safe.

DEDICATION

To all the spooky babes who love smut

Want a masked man to gut you with his cock?
Why not three masked men?
Why not three cocks?

Knock, knock
They're... cumming

CHAPTER 1

DAMIEN

"They're back," I announce, taking my seat at the head of the table.

Tension keeps the air heavy, the dark room illuminated only by flickering candles. All eyes are on me, trying to anticipate my next move.

"We're all aware that the displaying of a pig's head on a doorstep is the first step in the Hallowed Divine's ritual. This always takes place exactly one month before a full moon."

"How did they find out about her?" Asher asks.

Apollo chimes in. "It must be from someone they have on the inside."

BLOODBATH

"That's definitely possible," Jensen states from his position at my side.

"It was displayed on the doorstep at the sorority house, right?" Killian questions, scooting closer to the large wooden table. "How do we know for certain that Quinn is the target?"

"Coincidence?" Sam wonders.

I sigh. "Doubt it. That would be one hell of a coincidence. Besides, none of the other girls have ties to the Order like Quinn does."

"And her ties to those evil bastards, too. Let's not forget about that," Jensen scoffs.

"She's clearly the target." Micah lets out a sharp breath, running a shaky hand through his hair as he moves toward us. "It's too uncalculated for the Hallowed Divine to target one of her friends without knowing about her."

Suddenly the room is filled with chatter, every member talking amongst themselves about their opinions on the matter.

"Enough." My voice echoes against the walls. "We need to be even more cautious. I want her watched around the clock. If you spot them anywhere, near or far, kill on sight. I don't care who's watching. If you see them, you put a fucking bullet in their skull, gut them, whatever. You *take them out*. No hesitation."

"Damien," Killian cuts in. "Let's not get reckless here—"

"It's not up for debate."

"Kill on sight," Asher echoes warily.

Jensen places his hand on my shoulder and lowers his face beside my ear, speaking softly. "Don't we want to keep them alive? We could use them. Try to make them talk."

"I second that," Micah agrees, crowding my space. "We need to locate where they're hiding out. That's vital."

Shrugging them away, I pinch the bridge of my nose

between my fingers, trying to figure out the best approach.

Fuck. I hate that they're right.

I hate that my worst nightmare is coming true.

But most of all, I hate how I'm losing control so quickly. I've been losing sight of the bigger picture here. In their reality, this whole situation is much larger than Quinn, and although the Order has always been the most important part of my life, that's not the case anymore.

My little Quinn has secured that spot, surpassing everything else.

In their eyes, she's just a directive.

But in mine, she is the moon... the stars... sunlight... and oxygen all in one. I find shelter, warmth, and serenity in her arms. She is my turning point. My home.

My obsession.

Hell, she is *everything*.

Living without her is not an option.

CHAPTER 2

QUINN

"Give me all the details," Sarah exclaims, plopping down onto my bed and making herself comfortable while I begin to unpack. "Don't leave anything out."

"I'm not sure what you're referring to."

"Come on," she whines. "The last time I saw you was at the New Year's Eve party. You disappeared that night and have been avoiding all of us ever since."

Setting my cozy, winter sweaters neatly into my drawer, I roll my eyes. "I haven't been avoiding anyone."

"Oh, *pul-lease*."

BLOODBATH

"I swear. I've just been busy. They took me away for Christmas to the White Mountains."

"How was it?"

"It was so beautiful. We had a really nice time together. But when we got back to Salem and went to the New Year's Eve party…" I quiet, searching for the right words. I can never tell her how my boyfriends got revenge for me, so I go with something else. "It brought back a lot of memories."

"Good memories?"

Not so much.

Swallowing hard, I turn to face her with a reassuring grin. The royal blue masquerade mask comes to mind. "Let's just say I got my closure. I've moved on."

"I guess Eric packed up his shit and went to Italy."

My stomach sinks. "Oh?"

"Yeah. Nobody has heard from him since the party. All he left was a note."

"Crazy."

"So, your guys…" She raises an eyebrow, smiling. "Are you still seeing them? Has it been amazing?"

Every time I think about my masked men, I end up with butterflies, feeling flustered and giddy beyond belief. It sounds so corny, but it's true. I can't help the blush that settles on my cheeks. My heart skips a beat.

Being with Damien, Jensen, and Micah over the last few months has changed me for the better. They treat me like a queen.

As a result, I've found my confidence and self-worth.

"Yeah," I answer proudly, smiling from ear to ear. "We're still together. It's been great."

"So, is that polyamory?" I nod happily. "Damn. I can't imagine having three guys. I can hardly tolerate one."

With a laugh, I join her on the bed. "They're all so different from each other," I explain, hugging a pillow to my chest. "You know I've always been so glued to my work. Focused only on school. But ever since I met them on Halloween night, my life has changed. Everything feels different. *I* feel different."

She eyes me closely. "I'm not sure what you mean."

"I'm the happiest I've ever been."

"So what's the problem?"

"In the back of my mind, something just feels... off."

Sarah grimaces, trying to understand the meaning behind my words. "Everything's going good in your life. You're on cloud nine. What's so off about that?"

"Maybe this is the calm before the storm."

She rolls onto her back and giggles. "You worry too much."

"I know."

"Want some advice?"

"Please."

"Knock it the fuck off. Just soak in all the happiness your life has to offer... before everything turns to shit."

"Jeez, Sarah. Thanks for the reassurance."

"Anytime," she mutters as her phone goes off. "Jenna's FaceTiming."

"Oh boy."

"Sarah! Quinn!" Jenna exclaims, slurring her words.

"Hi, Jenna," I call out, leaning into view.

She smiles and stumbles over something. "Whoops! Party tonight?"

"I'd say the party has already started," Sarah playfully replies. "You're a mess."

"A *hot* mess," Jenna corrects. "But you still love me."

"Of course we do." I laugh. "You give us no choice."

Something slams against my window, making it rattle from the impact. The phone goes flying as Sarah lets out a panicked screech and I dive off the bed. Both the music and

BLOODBATH

Jenna's voice fades away as we try to collect ourselves, and I eventually notice a small crack in the glass. What the fuck?

When I finally find the strength to move, I crawl forward, peering out the large bay window with a racing heart. At first, nothing appears out of the ordinary.

I have a vantage point not only having my room on the second floor, but this old Victorian house sits on a hill overlooking the college town. I spot two of my sorority sisters making their way toward the path in the woods that leads to campus, the sound of their laughter drifting up to the window.

The other students I see are too far from the house to be the culprit, and I doubt it was the group of fraternity guys jogging by. It's clear their main focus is drawing out playful calls from my friends.

"Hello?" Jenna calls out to us. "Are you guys okay? What's going on?"

"Yeah, we're fine," Sarah confirms, still shaken as she reaches for her phone. "Something hit the window."

Finally, I notice the small black bird on the grass. It flaps its wings frantically, only to become completely still a moment later.

"Oh, no… It's a crow."

"Well, fuck." Sarah sighs. "That little shit scared the life out of me."

"Dumb bird," Jenna snorts.

"We can't just leave it there," I say.

Sarah appears beside me, stroking my shoulder as she peers outside. "Aw, babe," she coos, fighting laughter. "You're so sensitive. It's nature. Death is just a part of life."

With that, she leaves my room.

I wonder why I've been seeing so many crows over the last few weeks. Some say crows are a warning that death is near, while others say they are spiritual. Maybe I'm just paranoid and overthinking it. I'm anxious about this last semester of school.

But I keep having this feeling that something bad is coming.

A murder of crows in a nearby tree begin to call out for each other, ruffling their feathers and hopping from branch to branch.

Confusion floods through me. For some strange reason, it almost feels as if they're trying to communicate. Like some sort of warning. An *omen*.

My phone begins to ring. "Micah," I answer.

"Hi, baby," he murmurs. "You still unpacking?"

"I'm pretty much done. Just have a little bit left. Are you home?"

"Yeah, Damien and Jensen are out. Are you okay? You sound sad."

"A crow just flew into my window. I'm pretty sure it broke its neck or something. Should I bury it? Would that be weird?"

"I don't think so," he replies. "I used to have a crow visit me when I was younger."

"Really?"

"Yeah. It was when I was bouncing around foster homes. Kept finding me somehow. You know that if they make friends with you, they sometimes bring gifts?"

"No way." I laugh quietly. "Did you get one?"

"I did."

"What was it?"

"A used Q-Tip."

"Ew!" I gasp, on the verge of gagging. "That's so gross. Please tell me you didn't take it."

"Are you kidding, babe? I was the chosen one. I cherished that shit for years."

BLOODBATH

"You're disgusting."
He chuckles before letting out a small sigh. "I miss you."
"I miss you, too."
"Come sleep here tonight. I'll pick you up."
"Tempting, but I have class really early."
"I want you in my arms so bad. I need all the cuddles."
Suddenly, he FaceTimes me.

Soft natural light filters in through his window, casting a warm glow on his skin and bringing out the rich amber hues of his eyes. He's in bed, wrapped in a navy blue comforter, his head propped up by fluffy pillows. The scene on my phone looks so inviting. I wish I could step right through the screen to nuzzle my face in his sage green crew neck sweater.

"Fuck," he groans, sporting a crooked grin. "You're so damn beautiful. How'd I get so lucky?"
"Now I really wish I was there with you."
"Come cuddle."
"I mean, I could go for some food."
"Can I take you out to dinner?"
I smile from ear to ear. "That sounds really nice."

It's such a bitter January night. Fortunately, Micah has the heat blasting. He shuts the car door behind me and jogs around the front of the Jeep, hopping into the driver's seat with a childlike grin.

"Come here, baby," he says, taking my face between his hands.

He leans in, his lips brushing softly against mine. This is the way every girl yearns to be kissed. It feels like an out of body experience, like I've traveled to an entirely different universe, where it's just the two of us, floating. I'm completely lost in this moment, in *him*, and I wouldn't have it any other way.

CHAPTER 3

QUINN

Dinner was delicious, but I've worked up another appetite...
And it isn't for food.

Maybe it's from the way his hair is slicked back, the slight stubble on his face, or his *I really want to fuck you* eyes.

Whatever it is, I find myself clenching my thighs in search of relieving the ungodly ache. Beneath my skirt and tights, I'm wet, and when I place my hand on his thigh, I'm not surprised to feel his erection.

He pulls down a quiet side street, soft sounds escaping him while I work him through his jeans. I didn't think it was possible for him to grow harder, but here he is, proving me wrong.

Micah glances over at me briefly with heated eyes. "You want it?"

"Yes," I breathe eagerly.

"When?"

"Now."

"Here?"

I nod, heat rising in my cheeks.

He pulls over to the side of the road and places the car in park. Before he has the chance to fumble with his belt, I'm undoing it for him, and yanking the hem below his hips. The moment his cock springs free I take him into my mouth.

"Fuck," he moans heavily, running his hands through my hair.

Desperate and as feral as ever, I take him as deep as I can, gliding my tongue up and down his long length while pumping him with my hand.

"Ah, fuuuuck."

Bobbing my head, I suck him harder, coating every inch with saliva and tightening my grasp. I swear I'm about to come the second he reaches behind me and yanks down my tights, burying his hand between my legs, his fingers teasing my entrance.

"Goddamn, you're fucking wet."

With the head of his cock hitting the back of my throat, I gag.

"Good girl. Fucking choke on it," he commands, breathing heavily and thrusting deeper. "You're the cutest thing with a mouthful of my dick."

He traces his fingers over my clit, then presses down firmly, the friction sending sparks through me.

I moan fiercely, trembling.

Micah grips my hair tight, a brief sensation of pain ripping at my skull. He brings me down on his cock, pumping into my mouth repeatedly, cursing and groaning with each movement. He holds me in place, burying himself deep in my throat, stealing away my oxygen. I can't breathe. Can't think.

Tears stream down my face as I gag viciously, saliva pooling out of my mouth.

"That's my good little slut," he praises, bucking his hips and holding himself there, my lips stretched around his thickness. "Look at you, baby. I'm so. Fucking. Proud of you."

My heart thumps wildly, either from the loss of air or excitement.

Finally, he releases his tantalizing hold on the back of my head and strokes my face with his thumbs.

Still gasping for air, I work him with my hand, blinking up at him through tears.

His lips curl into a devious smirk. "Yeah? You like when I tell you that you're a good little slut for me? When I tell you how proud I am of you? When I steal your breath away and give you nothing but cock to choke on?"

My pussy spasms around his fingers as he buries them inside me. I cry out in desperation, needing so badly to come that I'm left trembling from his words, embarrassed to admit how drenched they've made me.

He grabs my jaw firmly and pries open my mouth with his thumb. "Answer me," he groans, his dick twitching in my grasp.

"Yes," I rush out pathetically, grinding against his hand as he fucks me with two fingers. "Yes, I fucking love it. All of it."

He bites his lip, watching me intently as I suck his thumb into my mouth. "You've been dying to ride my cock all night, haven't you?" I nod. "Is that what you want, baby girl?"

The tone of his voice alone almost makes me see stars.

BLOODBATH

He gathers more of my hair in his hand and I return to his pulsating cock, gliding my mouth up and down the full length of his shaft. "God damn," he groans, curling his fingers. I moan, sucking him hard. "Tell me what you want."

Releasing him with a wet plop, I look into his eyes and impatiently whimper, "I want you to fuck me. I want it so bad."

He fists his cock and removes his hand from my pussy. "Hop on."

Soft sounds escape him as he rolls back his seat. Without any hesitation, I kick off my boots and pull off my tights completely. Breathing hard, he yanks me onto his lap, my damp thighs now straddling his hips.

Taking my ass in his large hands, he brings me closer, staring straight into my soul as I lower myself onto him inch by inch. This position feels like heaven on earth. I can't help but cry out at the sensation of being so consumed.

I rock my hips, grinding myself against him while his thumb circles my clit. It's clear he's getting enjoyment out of giving me control, his eyes not leaving mine for even a second.

It doesn't even take me a full minute before I'm spiraling far over the edge. Raking my nails down Micah's ink-covered neck, my body convulses against his, my walls clutching him.

"Oh, fuck!" I scream, coming down harder, my bare ass smacking against the top of his thighs again and again. "Oh fuck, oh fuck… fuck!"

"That's my girl," he praises between clenched teeth, thrusting upwards to meet my rhythm. "Let me feel that pretty pussy suck at my cock."

He grips the back of my neck and brings me down forcefully, his forehead pressed against mine, and his eyes burning into my own.

"Say my name when you finish," he commands between thrusts. "Say my fucking name."

I rock my hips, arching my back as my head rolls. "Micah," I moan feverishly.

He grunts, pumping into me with strained breaths. "Fucking hell, baby. I love when my name falls from your lips."

"Micah," I cry out for him again.

"That all you got?"

"Micah!" I scream louder.

He slips his tongue into my mouth aggressively, one hand tangled in my hair and the other coming down forcefully on my ass.

He bucks his hips, sinking into me deeper. "Here?" he breathes softly.

"Right there, yes," I gasp into our kiss.

The passion between us builds, and when another wave of my orgasm claims me, he rests his face in the crook of my neck, trailing soft kisses down my throat.

"Keep coming for me," he whispers. "Give me another—"

The sound of a siren abruptly pulls us from the moment.

"Shit," he growls, catching a glimpse of flashing lights from behind us through the rearview mirror.

The both of us move fast, breathing harshly, our bodies covered in sweat. I'm back in my seat in the blink of an eye and Micah's erection is tucked back in his pants, straining uncomfortably.

After several police cars rush past us and disappear around the corner, I burst into laughter.

He stares at me incredulously. "I'm glad you think this is funny."

"I'm—I'm so sorry." I continue to belly laugh. "Oh my God. That scared the hell out of me! What a rush!"

BLOODBATH

He runs a hand through his hair.

"Are you going to get blue balls now?"

"Probably," he sighs.

"Isn't sex in a car illegal?"

He rubs at the big bulge in his pants. "Yup."

"I didn't even get to return the favor!" I reach for his thigh, tracing my hand over the outline of his erection. "Pull it back out. Let me suck it."

"I'm good, babe. All that matters is whether or not you got off," he replies with a smirk. "And given the fact your cum is all over my dick and thighs right now, I'd say mission accomplished."

"Can you imagine if you just got arrested for fucking me in public?"

"I mean," he says, shrugging it off, "I was more worried about you. I've done worse."

Goosebumps pebble on my skin.

Having sex in public is nothing like...

Murder.

I swallow hard.

Jenna may have been right about how the three of them are dangerous. I was naïve for a long time before I finally realized just how dangerous they truly are.

The darker part of myself simply doesn't care. They say love clouds your judgment, that it makes you do crazy things, things you'd never even dreamt of doing. They say love changes you. That it turns you into a different person. For a long time, I didn't believe it. I thought it was a bunch of hocus pocus. But now I'm a believer.

Although the voice in the back of my head taunts me every day.

Run, Quinn. They're dangerous. Darkness follows them everywhere. They kill people. One day, they're going to go down for all the horrific things they have done and keep doing. They're never going to stop. Run.

But... I'm not running.

Not unless I'm running with them.

On the way back to the sorority house, we end up driving past a house with several police cars parked out front. It takes my brain a second to register that it's the house where a suicide happened years ago. I remember my parents talking about how cheap it had sold for after the incident. The flashing red and blue lights are bright as we drive by slowly, taking in the scene of an older man and woman sobbing on the front lawn, having a quiet conversation with the officers.

"Oh shit," I say nervously. "That can't be good."

Micah reaches for my hand and holds it steadily on his lap for the rest of the ride back. He parks out front and walks me up the front steps. I can't tell if it's just in my head that his demeanor seems much different than earlier.

He has grown quiet, and there's a hint of apprehension in his eyes.

"You alright?" I ask, squeezing his hand.

He squeezes my hand in return. "I spent most of the night with you. I'm better than alright." I smile. "You sure you don't want to spend the night at our place?" he asks, tucking a strand of hair behind my ear.

"I have class early in the morning," I remind him. "Tomorrow night, maybe?"

"Come here." He brings me into a warm embrace, and I rest my face in his chest. "I miss you already."

BLOODBATH

My body relaxes as he rubs my back soothingly.

"I wonder what was going on back there."

"Where?"

"At the house with all the cops."

He tenses against me, tracing gentle circles with his fingertips on the small of my back. "I'm not sure."

"I've heard some horror stories about that house," I tell him, a chill shooting down my spine at the thought.

"Like what?"

"That someone died there. Don't they call it the suicide house?"

"Something like that." He displays a subtle grin when I step back, so subtle it almost looks forced. "I hate that you have to wake up so early. It's cold as shit and I want to use your body for warmth."

With a giggle, I draw him closer. "See you tomorrow," I say, standing on my toes and pressing my lips against his.

He nods, his fingers curling around the nape of my neck and holding me in place. I lean into him, slipping my tongue past the seam of his lips. My stomach flutters and my arms find their way around his neck, my fingers combing through his hair. I catch the low groan of satisfaction he releases in my mouth, his hands roaming down my hips and gripping my ass.

"Goodnight, baby," he whispers, drawing back his head and looking into my eyes. He takes a moment, searching for the right words. With a sigh, he leans down and kisses me tenderly, caressing my cheekbone with the back of his fingers. "I hope you know how much you mean to me."

"I do," I breathe into our kiss.

"You mean the world to us," he murmurs, kissing me passionately. "I hope you know by now that we'd do anything for you." My heart races. "You do know that, right?" He takes my face between both his hands and stares into my eyes with admiration.

"Yes," I whisper, so softly I'm not sure he hears it.

"Good," he breathes, leaning down and kissing the tip of my nose. "I love you. Get some sleep."

Micah freezes, his eyes growing wide as shock spreads across his face.

My heart skips a beat, my mouth falling open.

"I-I mean—I'm—" he stutters. "I'm sorry. It wasn't supposed to happen that way. It slipped out..."

"Micah," I murmur, my hands trembling against his chest.

"Fuck, I'm sorry—"

"I love you, too."

"Wha—You do?" he asks, childlike, his eyes lighting up in ways I've never seen before. "Quinn Rowland loves me?"

"Yes," I confess.

Suddenly his lips are firm on mine, both sensual and tender. I'm consumed with intense sensations, bouncing from nervous excitement, exhilaration, and vulnerability, but somehow, there's no fear.

Not even a hint.

I've never felt so sure.

He softly traces my cheek with his thumb, his head tilting to the side and deepening the kiss. A deep hum escapes him as he pulls my body into him, his tongue thrashing against mine. My knees grow weaker by the second. My hands explore his biceps and shoulders while his fingers run through my hair, the passionate and sexual tension building between us.

My body quivers in response to his gentle caresses. His cedar scented cologne and the peppermint taste of his lips sends my senses into overdrive. Our breathing quickens, the desire of one another intensifying. With each stroke of our wandering fingertips, the urgency between us grows.

Micah holds me close, his large hand trailing up my spine to cradle the back of my neck. He pulls away briefly, gazing into my eyes with admiration.

"You're the first person to ever tell me they love me."

"And this is the first time I've ever said it to anyone," Micah replies. "Let me try this again."

He moves me backward until my back is flush with the door, his lips meeting mine once more. An ache settles between my damp thighs as desire continues to spread throughout my body like a wildfire.

"I'm in love with you, Quinn. You're perfect for me, in every way," he whispers, capturing my bottom lip with his teeth.

I plant a small kiss on his jaw. "You're perfect for me, too."

"You're mine forever." He caresses my face with the back of his hand, his eyes eagerly exploring mine.

"And you're mine."

"I should go. I can feel the worst of my corniness getting ready to break free."

I laugh quietly. "But that's one of my favorite things about you."

"Fuck, babe. You're biting your lip and it's…" he hesitates, taking in a shallow breath, shifting his stance. "I really need to go do something about this."

"Don't go," I whisper, my fingers roaming through his hair as I bring him closer, refusing to let go.

"Feel what you do to me." He takes my hand and guides it down to the large bulge in his pants. "Loving you makes my dick so fucking hard."

I moan, fighting back the urge to strip off my clothes right here and now, even in mid-January while there's still fresh snow covering the ground.

"If I don't leave right this second, baby, I'm going to end up bending you over and taking you from behind, right here," he warns, staring at me through heated eyes.

Leaning forward, I press my body into him. "Do it."

"Yeah?" he asks, the corners of his lips tugging into a wicked grin. A small groan of sexual frustration escapes him. "Don't tempt me. You know I will. Or you can just sneak me upstairs."

"No guys allowed, sorority rules—"

"Then let me give you another." He reaches down between us to slip his hand between my legs.

Spreading my legs slightly, I inhale a small breath, quivering against his touch. His lips meet mine in a hungry kiss. He lightly grazes my clit with his fingertips, not quite making full contact. The edging is absolute torture.

But my head rolls back along with my eyes just from the teasing and anticipation. His warm mouth feels like fire on my skin as he trails soft kisses along my throat. He licks, nips, and bites his way to my collarbone, his finger teasing my entrance. The heel of his palm brushes against my clit as he sinks two fingers inside me.

I whimper, my back arching from the door. Even while the bitter air nips at my skin, I've started sweating, my endorphins raging. He works my clit with his thumb and pumps into me deeper, curling his fingers and stroking my most sensitive spot. My thighs lock around his wrist and my body stiffens.

He takes hold of my jaw with his free hand and demands eye contact, his gaze searching my face, studying my every response to his touch. Right on cue, my breathing hitches in my throat as the roughness of his palm grazes my swollen clit.

"Micah," I breathe deeply.

"I love the way your cheeks turn red," he observes, working his fingers deeper inside me, quickening his thrusts.

BLOODBATH

"You blush so easily." I buck my hips forward, matching his movements, desperate for another inevitable orgasm. "Grind that pussy against my hand like a good fucking girl."

I continue riding his hand, my arms around his neck and nails digging into his broad shoulders. My jaw drops as my peak rapidly approaches. He knows just how to touch me.

"Give it to me, Quinn," he orders, firmly gripping my jaw. "Come all over my fingers. Give me something to taste for the ride home. I'm starving."

I'm instantly swept away, a pleasure so intense my knees unlock, and I nearly sink to the ground.

"Mmm... Just like that."

Micah hugs me against him, watching in awe as I come undone, my pussy clenching tight around his fingers.

He leans down, eying me closely, his lips brushing my ear. "I love when you fall apart for me," he says, before slipping his fingers into his mouth with a hungry groan and heady eyes. He opens the front door for me and smacks my ass as I step inside. "Sleep well, baby."

CHAPTER 4

MICAH

When I arrive back at the apartment, it feels like I'm walking on air. I drop my keys on the table beside the front door and kick off my boots, still feeling Quinn's lips on mine. It's the first time I've ever told a woman I love her.

It's the first time I've told anyone that ever, actually.

Steam from the shower fills the bathroom as I strip off my clothes. The hot water feels incredible on my skin. I roll my neck, lathering the shampoo through my hair and picturing the sweet look on Quinn's face when the words slipped from my lips.

BLOODBATH

She is the most amazing woman I've ever known. Despite everything life has thrown at her, she still manages to see the beauty in some of the darkest moments.

I just hope she can still find it in her to smile when she finds out who she truly is. Who *we* are. Why we've come into her life. I hope she'll be able to understand that yes, she may have been an order at first, but she has become so much more than that.

Maybe it wasn't the smartest choice on our end to become so deeply involved, but I don't regret it for one second.

I love her with everything in me, every ounce of my fucking soul, and because of that I will do anything in the world for her. All she has to do is tell me what she needs, and I will oblige, no questions asked. I'd burn the whole world into ashes for her.

My dick grows hard. Stroking myself tenderly from tip to base, I plant my free hand against the cold tile wall, keeping myself steady as I work my cock faster, pumping into my fist again and again.

The abrupt sound of the shower door opening from behind me makes me jump.

"Fuck," I exhale, blinking past small droplets of water. "Caught me off guard."

Jensen strips off his clothes then enters the shower, shutting the glass door behind him.

"I didn't expect you home this soon," I moan, stroking myself faster.

He approaches me without a word. I look into his hazel eyes and my heart pounds. "Need some help with that?" he finally asks, sinking to his knees.

"Sure. It's going to be a quick one."

He wraps his fingers around my width and takes my cock all the way into the back of his throat. I see stars, my mouth falling open.

"Oh, fuck," I whimper, gripping the back of his head and shoving myself deeper. "All night. All fucking night... I've needed this... Needed to come so fucking bad. Fuck, Jensen... *fuck.*"

He gags violently, bobbing his head and running his tongue up and down the length of my shaft. I thrust into the warmth, gripping his wet hair and tugging taut on the strands.

He slips his hand behind me and teases my ass with his finger.

"Yes," I groan, my voice hoarse and desperate. "Ah, fuck—"

He sinks his lean finger inside me, curling slightly and stroking all the right spots. Unable to hold back, I come undone immediately, exploding into his mouth and whimpering loudly through my orgasm.

He spits my cum into his palm and lubes his cock. "Turn around," he instructs, bending me over as I take hold of the handrail.

Jensen enters me forcefully, jolting my body forward with each thrust. His fingertips dig into my hips while he holds me steady, his hips slamming against my ass with each stroke. He fucks me without emotion. The sounds of our skin smacking, groans and uneven breaths echo against the walls.

"Mine," he grunts between thrusts, slowing his pace unexpectedly. "Such a needy boy. You're so desperate for cock, aren't you, slut?"

"Yes," I breathe out through the steady rise and fall of my chest. "Don't stop."

"Go on," he urges between thrusts. "Tell me what you want."

"Faster."

His hand trails up the length of my back. He grips the back of my neck, getting a better grip on me, and then slams into me repeatedly. I push back against him, craving every inch.

"Oh, fuck," I call out. "That feels so fucking good."

He wraps my hair around his wrist and pulls tight, the front of his body flush with my back. "You want it harder?"

I nod, trembling with desperation.

"Fucking. Say. It."

The hot stream of water strikes the skin of my shoulder blades with a light, pattering force, along with his fingertips exploring the contours of my body. I shiver from his soothing touch. Even with him taking me roughly, he's my oasis.

The top of his thighs slap against my ass with each stroke. I lose myself in the feeling of being stretched, entirely consumed with his thickness. Suddenly, he becomes still, edging me, his lips brushing my shoulder.

"Please," I beg. "I fucking want it. Fuck me harder."

He slams into me punishingly, pain shooting through my skull as he tugs on my hair, sending me into a state of pure bliss. Bent over with my face pressed against the wall, I take him at a different angle, causing his dick to hit the spot that makes my eyes roll back in ecstasy. My body vibrates with pleasure and my knees give out for the briefest of moments.

Jensen sneaks his arm around my waist, holding me upright while giving himself better leverage. He quickens his pace, thrusting into me in deep, aggravated bursts.

"Jesus, fuck," he moans harshly. "Your ass is gripping my cock so fucking tight. I'm gonna come. I'm gonna fucking come, Micah—"

The bathroom door opens, but Jensen doesn't slow.

"Did you tell him yet?" Damien asks impatiently.

"Fuck, Micah. FUCK."

"For fuck's sake, Jensen," he snaps. "Getting off is more important to you? Hurry the fuck up."

"Fuuuuck," Jensen bites out, spilling himself inside my ass

with one final thrust.

Tuning the both of them out, I come... *hard...* riding the waves of bliss as Jensen buries his fingertips into my hips.

He groans, slipping out of me and bringing his palm down firmly on my ass.

"Well don't just stand there and look pretty, Damien," I smugly say, washing the rest of the shampoo out of my hair. "What's going on?"

"There was a second girl reported missing tonight," Damien explains.

Shit. My mind immediately goes to the cops parked outside the house earlier. Coincidence?

I glare at Jensen and give him a gentle shove. "What the fuck, man? You don't think you should have mentioned that first?"

He eyes me cautiously while lathering his body. "What difference would it have made? We knew this was coming. Plus, you had your cock in your hand and that look in your eye. You really expected me to not suck it?"

I snort.

"Cute. Love the banter, really, but it's time to talk business."

"Discuss away, then." My tone drips in sarcasm. "I'm listening."

He shoots me a dirty look in return.

Rolling my eyes, I step out of the shower and wrap a towel around my waist. "Okay, fine. Now I am."

"Can you just give me a minute? I'll be right out," Jensen says.

Damien sits against the edge of the sink, lost in his thoughts.

Leaning against the counter beside him, I lower my gaze to the floor. "I saw Quinn tonight."

Damien doesn't say anything.

"How is she?" Jensen asks. "I haven't talked to her since our FaceTime earlier."

"A bird blew into her window and broke its neck, and then I took her out to dinner."

"Death made her hungry? Interesting," Jensen jokes. It doesn't land.

When I shift my gaze, I realize Damien has gone quiet because he's been staring at me. He gives me the up and down, his main focus being my lower half. More specifically, the bulge beneath my towel.

"Want some?" I tease.

Damien cocks his head to the side, his eyes drifting from my waist to my eyes. "You'd like that, wouldn't you?" he challenges, wetting his lips with the tip of his tongue.

Standing face to face with him, my palms grow clammy, an unexpected fluttering sensation arising deep in my stomach. With my gaze locked on his mouth, I watch the way he presses his teeth into his bottom lip. I'd be lying if I said I wasn't intrigued by the thought of it, the pure curiosity of what it would feel like to cross that line.

For fun, of course.

"I told Quinn I love her," I reveal.

His smirk falls away, the playfulness between us dissipating.

"It slipped out, and I told her I love her, yet here I am," I hesitate, forcing a bitter laugh. "Still hiding shit and lying to her face."

A wave of guilt eats at me.

"Micah," Damien begins, cupping my jaw with his hand and making me look at him, "we knew what we were getting ourselves into. We crossed the line by making this personal. We knew her role in all this shit—her place in the society, that her birth mother gave her up to protect her from that sadistic prick. We took an oath and at the time, it was for a good reason. We've had her best interest at heart since day one."

"That doesn't make it right," I argue. "She's the only one who doesn't know. It's not fucking fair."

"No," he admits, letting his hands fall from my face as he steps back. "It's not. That's why we're going to tell her the truth."

Jensen steps out of the shower with shocked eyes, too caught up in the moment to even bother grabbing a towel. "And... our orders?"

"Fuck our orders," Damien shoots back.

"She doesn't even know she's adopted," I let out warily.

"Felicity wanted it this way for a reason," Damien reminds us. "But that was back when the Hallowed Divine didn't know Quinn even existed. That was the point, to hide her from those bastards. But now they know, and our safest bet is to come clean. She deserves to know."

"I agree," I say.

"Me, too. How does Killian feel about this? The Order?" Jensen wonders, folding his arms across his toned chest. "Not that I honestly give a fuck."

"Peter isn't in command anymore, so Killian can't say shit," I press.

"Things change. Time does that," Damien says, glancing at me briefly. "We can finish this conversation after I return his call." His eyes narrow as he strides past us, shoving a towel against Jensen's chest. "In the meantime, will you put some damn clothes on? It's staring at me."

"Don't be envious. I was born this way."

Damien ignores his sarcasm entirely and dismisses himself from the bathroom.

"So, you told her you love her," Jensen pries, attempting to sound casual while he wraps the towel around his hips.

BLOODBATH

Except there's just something about his tone that throws me off. "Did she say it back?"

With a slight nod, I begin brushing my teeth. "Shockingly, yes. I feel like I'm dreaming."

"Damn. That's big, Micah."

"I know," I mumble.

"I'm happy for you." I watch his reflection through the mirror. Surveying my face, he doesn't say anything further. He just watches me with a hint of curiosity building in his eyes.

"Well?" I spit out.

"Well, what?"

"You look like you want to ask me something," I observe, rinsing my mouth with water before turning to meet his gaze. "So ask away."

"Okay," he says bleakly, approaching me slowly. He presses the front of his body against mine, forcing my ass against the counter. "Is this the first time you've told someone you love them?"

"Yeah."

He lifts his hand beside my face, allowing it to linger there without making even the slightest contact. When I sense his uncertainty, I circle my fingers around his wrist and lean into his touch, resting my face in his palm.

A small breath escapes him as his thumb traces the contour of my cheekbone in small circles. "Do you think it's possible to love two people at once?" he asks.

"Definitely possible."

He arches a brow, leaning closer, his breath lightly fanning my lips. "You sure?"

"I'm sure."

"How?"

"Personal experience."

His eyes narrow. "Oh?"

"You asked if this is the first time I've told someone I love them, not if it's my first time falling in love."

His body relaxes against mine. It's been complete hell holding this inside for all this time. There's this strong feeling of relief. It's crazy that after all these years, we've never spoken this intimately. He's always had a wall up between us, and now here he is, allowing any remaining pieces to crumble.

"This is long overdue, don't you think?" I question. "Are you going to make me say it?"

"No," he replies, his voice soft and comforting. "You don't have to say anything. I can feel it. I always have."

His lips collide with mine not even long enough for me to blink before he draws back, breaking our kiss. A rush of emotions surge through my body.

Without saying another word, I clutch the nape of his neck and pull him into me, sealing this moment with a kiss.

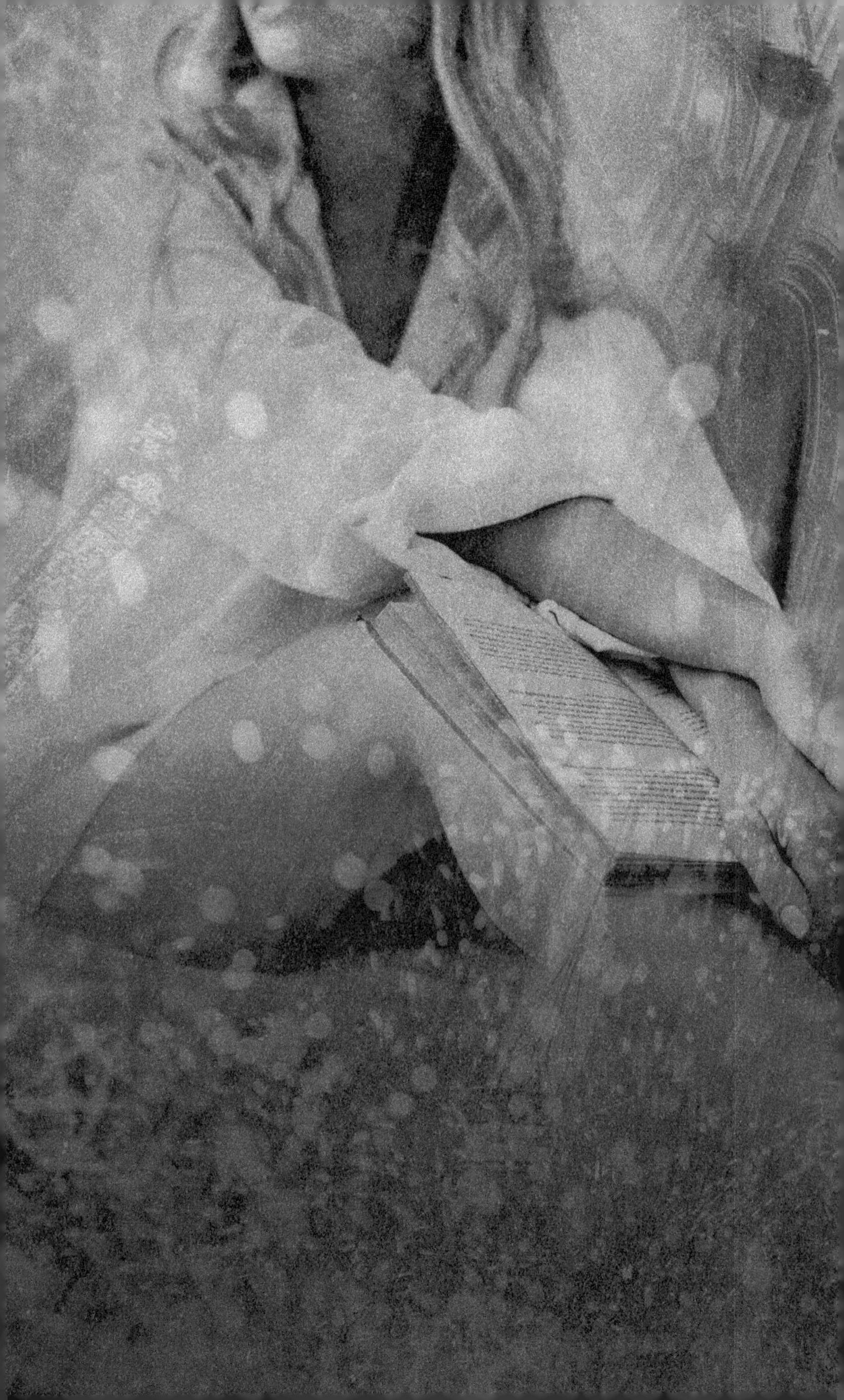

CHAPTER 5

QUINN

The sky is a pale blue hue, and although the sun is visible, it's lacking warmth. The frigid air bites at my skin as I nuzzle deeper into my winter coat, walking through campus until I stumble upon my favorite coffee shop.

I rush inside, seeking refuge from the icy air. I've always adored the coziness of this place, the soft lighting, and plush sofas, but most importantly, the heavenly smell of the coffee beans. I loosen my scarf and breathe in the freshly baked pastries, my mouth watering.

Jenna and Georgia wave me over to our usual table,

seeming like they're in some sort of hurry. I stride over quickly and take my seat.

"Cold brew, because you're fucking *nuts*," Jenna says, sliding my cup in front of me.

Georgia laughs, blowing on her steaming hot cup of coffee, attempting to cool it down. "I don't know how you drink iced when it's this cold outside."

"Don't act like I'm the only one," I retort, gesturing around the room. "Tell me you weren't born in New England without telling me you weren't born in New England."

"Did you guys see the fucking syllabus?" Jenna asks.

"Yup," I sigh, taking a long, much needed gulp of my coffee. "It's insane."

"I don't know how I'm going to make it this semester," Georgia sighs. "I just want to be done with it already."

I laugh. "Babe, it's literally our first day back."

"Our first day back and I was falling asleep during the cardiac lecture."

Jenna leans back against the seat with a devious smirk. "We gonna party it up tonight or what?"

"And I'm the one who's nuts," I mutter.

She rolls her eyes at me in response. "Tell me you're boring without telling me you're boring."

"I'm probably going to hang out in the library for the next few hours," I tell them. "My next class isn't until six."

Georgia frowns. "Yikes."

"Drinks after class then?" Jenna asks.

"If by drinks you mean Redbull or more coffee," I counter. "Otherwise, I think I'll pass."

"Same," Georgia agrees, resting her face on her arm. "I'm already exhausted. I can't wait to go to bed."

"Whatever then," Jenna snarls.

Georgia scrolls through her phone casually for a moment

before gasping abruptly. "Shit. Did you guys hear about the missing girls?" she asks.

I frown, concerned.

"No," Jenna and I reply in unison.

"Okay, so, crazy shit. A girl was reported missing about a week ago. Her family was on the news asking for any tips. Well, apparently a second girl has gone missing. Her parents reported it last night after not hearing from her for a few days. I guess none of her friends have heard from her either."

"That's terrifying," Jenna gasps.

"Mhm. Both girls are from Salem and one of them goes to school here. Word has already started to spread. I'm surprised you haven't heard."

"Wait," I rush out, thinking back to last night when I saw the police in front of that house. "I saw cops last night when we drove down Elm street."

"Did you?" Jenna questions.

"Yeah. They looked really distraught and the officers seemed to be consoling them. Do we know who the girl is?"

"Juniper St. Graves."

Jenna takes a quick sip of her coffee. "Hmm. Never heard of her."

"She's a sophomore here," Georgia says, pulling up an article on her phone and showing us the photo of her. "I don't think I've ever seen her around."

"Me either," I reply somberly. "That's so sad. I hope they find her. The other girl, too."

"Same. It's so awful. You know I'm really into true crime and shit, but I hope we don't have a serial killer in town or something. Two missing girls so close together?"

"Yeah. That is a bit bizarre," I agree.

"I know for sure I'm never walking on campus alone. Not until we have answers at least."

BLOODBATH

"I'm not scared," Jenna states as she stands, brushing her hair behind her shoulder. "Be safe, babes. Don't forget your pepper spray."

Georgia shakes her head as we watch our friend hurry out of the coffee shop. "She's something else."

"Right?" I scoff, peering out the window, my eyes taking in Jenna as she passes by.

The second she leaves my view, something catches my attention almost instantly. My gaze locks in on a hooded figure. They stand across the street, almost appearing statuesque as they stare straight in our direction, with squared shoulders and bulky arms pressed firm against their sides.

At first, I don't think anything of it. This time of day is usually busy with college students roaming around campus. Someone standing by the bus station isn't necessarily a call for concern. Maybe they are waiting for their friends or simply trying to pass the time by while they wait for their classes to begin.

But there's something oddly familiar about their presence and the way I feel like they're watching... *me*. Even with the distance between us, and the black hoodie paired with a thick leather jacket, there's this gut feeling that they are no stranger.

Georgia snaps her fingers at me. "Earth to Quinn?"

"Uh, yeah..." I say, my voice trailing off as I catch her eyes burning with curiosity.

"What are you staring at?"

"You see that person by the bus stop?"

She looks through the window, and with a slight nod, replies, "Yeah."

"Doesn't it look like he's watching us?"

After squinting my eyes in hopes of getting a better look, I begin to suspect it's Damien.

After a minute of the both of us staring absently at the

figure, I pull out my phone and send my boyfriend a text.

Quinn: Does watching me get you off?

Damien: Always, little Quinn.

By the time I look up from my phone, he's no longer there.
"Where did he go?" I ask.

Georgia shrugs, scrolling through social media. "Not sure. I'm going to order another coffee. Want a refill?"

"I'm okay."

She heads toward the register at the front of the coffee shop.

When I look back to the window, my breathing hitches. The glass is fogged up in one specific spot, as if someone was just standing there. I shift in my seat, a subtle shiver traveling down my spine. If that's the case, they had to have been peering in.

"Do you want some company in the library?" Georgia asks when she returns.

"Yes, please. I don't know why I'm getting so spooked."

She winches, her attention glued to the screen of her phone. "Jesus. I'm really surprised you haven't seen any of this on social media."

"I haven't been on much lately," I say. "Spare me the details. I'm already freaked out enough as it is."

She glances up at me and sighs. "Let's just get our minds off it. I have two hours to kill."

"I mean, we don't have to spend the time in the library... Power nap?"

"Fuck yeah," she agrees.

We scoot out our chairs and exit the cafe, the icy air

greeting us as we step outside. As we begin to walk past the window, I stop dead in my tracks.

A message has been left on the fogged up glass.

Hi LQ

"Oh my God," I stammer, grabbing Georgia's wrist.

"What?"

"Read it!"

She leans forward, closely observing each letter. "Okay?"

"Little Quinn," I urge impatiently, hating how it's just an inside thing between my boyfriends and I.

Georgia grins, catching me off guard with laughter. "Oh, come on," she dismisses. "LQ could literally mean anything."

With narrowed eyes, I focus on the message once more. My gut is screaming that this was no coincidence. Everything about this feels personal... like it was meant just for me.

"Is that even a Q? Looks like an O to me."

"That is definitely not an O," I press, desperately scanning our surroundings.

"Alright. Let's say someone left this for you to find."

I swallow. "Okay..."

"Why? What's the point?"

"I don't know. To scare me?"

"But, why? Who would want to scare you?" With a defeated sigh, I meet her gaze. "See?" she questions, placing a comforting hand on my shoulder. "We're okay. Anxiety sucks ass. I fucking hate it. Your brain is just playing tricks on you."

I nod, leaning my head on her shoulder.

Tearing my gaze away from the message, I walk past the coffee shop, bus stop, and college students, hoping she's right.

All while wondering whose hand was behind it... because it wasn't Damien's handwriting.

Or Jensen's.

Not even Micah's.

MOLLY DOYLE

Class wasn't as bad as I thought it would be. Time went by faster than I expected, and by the time I'm walking back to the sorority house it's a little before seven thirty. Streetlamps guide my path as darkness falls.

The buildings and landmarks I encounter during the day look much different at night. There's this peaceful calm that washes over me, the stars twinkling above me along with a gentle glow.

It'll be a full moon before we know it.

There's still a handful of students roaming around, and I make sure to stick to well-lit areas, especially after hearing about those missing girls earlier today. I will never forget my pepper spray moving forward.

My favorite song, "Rain" by Sleep Token, plays through my earbuds, drowning out all other sounds. It's probably not the smartest idea considering I'm walking alone, but at the same time, Salem is my home. I still feel safe here, even amongst the hidden corridors and shadows.

Out of the blue, a general feeling of unease settles over me. It's the same spine-chilling feeling I got last semester, right before we were pranked with the pig's head on our doorstep. I slow my pace, removing the earbud from my left ear.

I take in a deep breath as my heart sinks into my stomach. Then I spin around quickly, eyes wide and my body completely on alert and...

Nothing is there.

Just silence.

I scan the area for any threats, my heart pounding through

BLOODBATH

my ribcage. Am I losing my mind? Surely I must be losing it. Right?

My gut is screaming at me that *they are there*. I have the sudden urge to run as fast as I can, but I'm paralyzed, my feet bolted to the pavement.

It's as if everything has become still. I look around at my surroundings more carefully, a growing sense of defenselessness coming over me. Nothing appears to be out of the ordinary. I watch a guy disappear behind a gate. There's someone else across the street, but he appears to be in his own head, his gaze fixed on his phone.

I sigh, mentally scolding myself for being so paranoid.

Nobody is watching me.

Taking longer strides, my footsteps become louder against the pavement, but they're not the only thing I hear. The sound of my rapid pulse swishes in my ears, and I can hear the uneven pattern of my breaths. The feeling of being watched returns with a vengeance.

Every instinct warns me to take off running, goosebumps prickling across my skin. Even with the icy air nipping at my face, I can feel myself sweating. The shadows surrounding me take on a life of their own, and before I can even make sense of it, I'm running down the sidewalk as fast as I can.

Until I trip on a crack in the pavement and come down hard on my knees and palms. I gasp for air, fighting through the pain while I stumble back to my feet.

That's when I finally see a tall, dark figure looming in the distance. I begin to wonder if my mind is just playing tricks on me.

But it's not.

This is real.

I *am* being watched.

They draw my attention like a magnet, an invisible force

pulling me in. There's far too much distance between us for me to make out any details, but their presence feels unfamiliar. They stand out amongst the outline of trees, and even though I'm alone and completely helpless, I don't have a voice. I want to scream, but I can't.

They begin to wave.

A shudder runs through me. Are they seriously waving right now? Are they trying to be funny? Are they taunting me?

I step back, trying to make sense of their friendly yet creepy gesture.

Although just as quickly as the dark silhouette appeared, they vanish into the night.

With a shaky breath, I pull out my phone.

Quinn: You guys are such pranksters

Damien: You're so random today. But yeah... we are

I roll my eyes.

Once I get back to the sorority house I hop straight into the shower, unable to shake off the strange encounter I had this morning. I know that it's unlikely that my mind was playing tricks on me, but I try to convince myself anyways.

Georgia was right.

Georgia was right.

Georgia was...

As I crawl into bed, I let out a deep breath, wishing for my exhaustion to return. I had no energy all day, up until about thirty minutes ago. Now, I can't seem to get rid of the adrenaline that's still surging through me.

Even in the darkness, something on my pillow catches my eye. A small, black piece of paper neatly folded. I reach

BLOODBATH

toward my nightstand to turn on the lamp for better visibility. There's a message in gold writing.

Knock, knock.

My blood runs ice cold.

What the hell?

What is with all these creepy gestures?

A soft tap on my window catches me off guard. I crawl out of bed and draw the curtains to the side, scanning the area cautiously. I'm unable to find any answers at first. Maybe another crow flew into my window? Was it my imagination?

Damien must be playing a trick on me. It seems like something he would do.

Searching once more, I nearly jump out of my own skin. A dark figure stands motionless in the shadows.

Before any alarm bells are set off in my head, the glow from the moon reveals a mask. I grin, rolling my eyes. Finally, I'm able to relax. It must have been him watching me on campus earlier. He's toying with me. I wave Damien up, even though I know this is breaking the rules of the sorority. I could get in a lot of trouble.

He shakes his head.

Doing a quick glance around so nobody walking past can see me, I lift my shirt, pressing my bare chest against the cold glass. My nipples pucker immediately. My breath fogs up the window as I lean closer, watching the slight tilt of his head as he takes in the sight of my full breasts on perfect display just for him.

Even though he can't see it, I write *hi* in the fogged up area.

I feel so naughty trying to get a reaction out of him. All I want is to feel his warm masculine body pressed against mine. It's been days since he's last been inside me. A playful idea comes to mind. I hold up a finger, gesturing for him to wait for a second before retrieving my phone from my nightstand and dialing his number.

Phone sex, it is.

Wetness pools between my thighs as I imagine his hard, thick cock slick with desire.

I'm ready to tease.

He watches me from below. This masked stalker and innocent college student roleplay drives me wild. I slip my hand in my pants and decide to give him a special show, moaning quietly as I trace my clit with my fingers.

"I was just thinking about you, princess," Damien answers after one ring. "I can't sleep."

My mind draws a blank. Suddenly, I freeze, trying to comprehend how he answered the phone when both of his hands are clearly secured in his pockets.

"Your texts have been so weird all day. Are you good?"

"How are you doing that?" I wonder.

He pauses briefly. "Doing what?"

"You answered the phone without even touching it…"

There's another pause before he responds, an edginess to his tone. "Babe, what are you talking about?"

"That's not you, is it?" I ask, although in my head, I already know the answer.

It wasn't him at the coffee shop.

It wasn't him on campus.

It wasn't him who left the note.

And it's certainly not him who is standing below my window… watching.

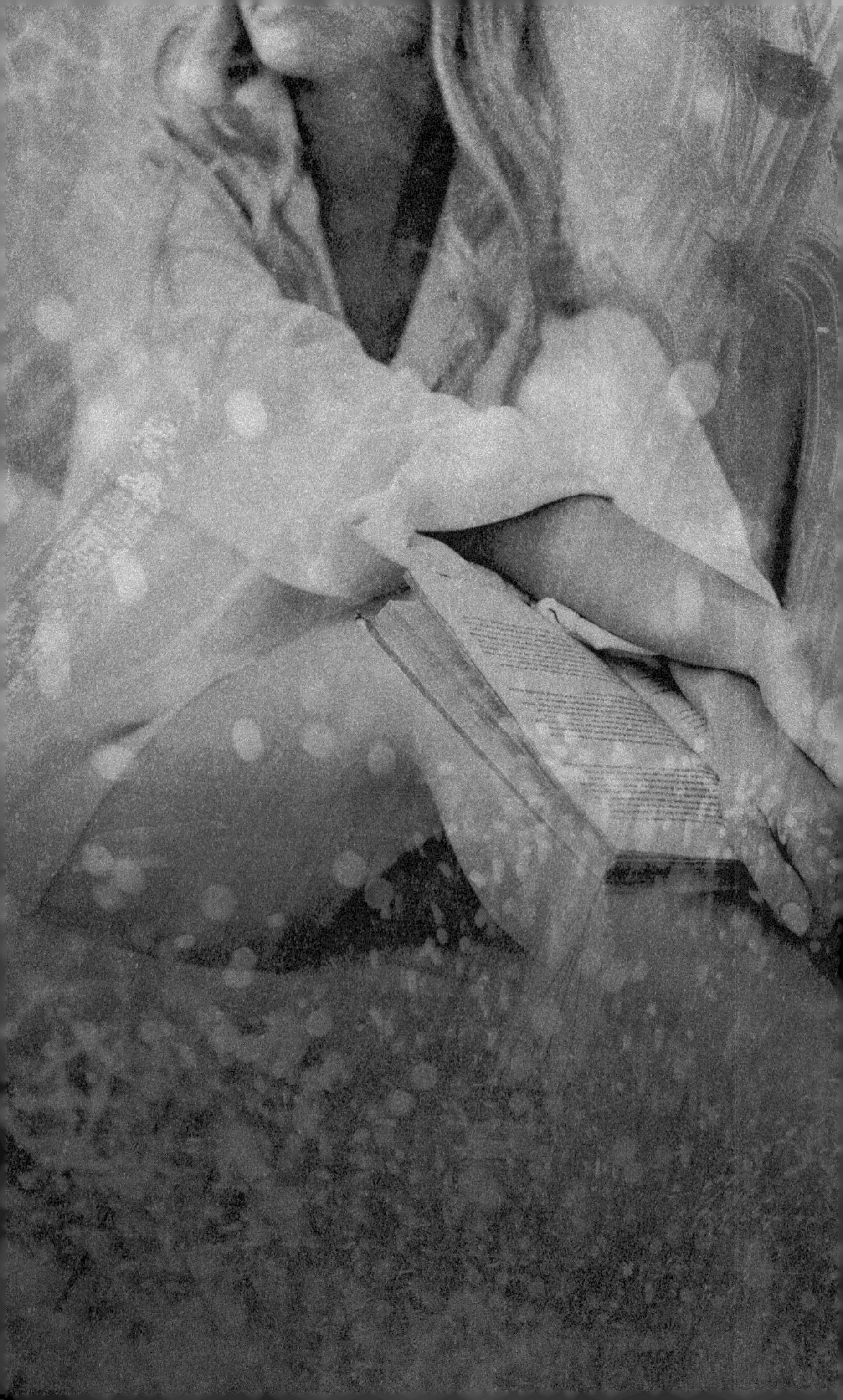

CHAPTER 6

QUINN

"Is she okay?" I hear Jensen ask.

"What's going on?" Micah demands.

"Quinn? Quinn?"

"There's someone standing outside my window. He's wearing a mask. *Your* mask. But it's red… with devil horns."

"We're on our way," he reassures me. Even with the closed window and heat blasting, a chill travels straight through my body. "Are you in your room?"

I nod.

"Quinn?" he urges.

"Yes, I'm in my room."

"Lock your door."

I rush toward it, turning the lock with trembling hands. "It's locked."

"That's my girl," Damien praises.

"Quinn." Micah's voice sounds rough through the receiver. "You're okay, baby. We're on our way to you now."

The Jeep's engine roars to life.

"I was in the shower… I came back to my room and found a note on my pillow…" My heart accelerates. "That wasn't you?"

"Call Asher, now," Damien orders.

"I've already got him on the line," Jensen answers.

"What did the note say?" Micah asks.

"Knock, knock."

"This isn't the time for jokes—"

"No. That's what the note says."

Everyone starts talking all at once. More voices than I can count. I lose track of the conversations almost immediately. My head is spinning.

"Where the fuck are you?"

"You're supposed to be on watch."

"Did you find them?"

An unfamiliar voice speaks up. "I'm still here. There are no threats. I'm literally out front—"

"Someone is standing outside her window, Asher," Micah presses.

"They got into the house," Jensen snaps.

"Who is that?" I question.

There's not a single word in response. Silence takes over, and it takes me a few seconds before I realize they've muted themselves.

"Damien? Jensen? Micah? Hello?"

"We're still here," Micah replies, and although he's trying to hide it from me, there's an urgency to his tone.

"Who was that? Who is Asher?"

More silence.

"What the hell is going on?" I demand, desperate for an answer and hating how it feels like they're keeping something from me. They must know who the person outside is and why they're here. The fact that they aren't filling me in tells me it's serious. I hug my knees to my chest, staring toward my window. "I really don't want to be alone right now. Someone was watching me earlier. I assumed it was you and didn't really think anything of it, but now I'm freaking out. I don't understand what is happening—"

"You're staying with us tonight," Damien declares. "We're about five minutes out. Our friend is going to stay with you until we get there."

"Your friend? What?"

"Asher," he says. "You can trust him. He's my cousin."

There's a soft knock on my door. "What the hell? He's here already? Is that him knocking?"

"Yes, that's him," Jensen answers.

"If you don't feel comfortable letting him in your room, that's fine," Damian says, "but he's going to stay with you until we get there. Okay?"

"Okay." Once I pull on some sweatpants and a hoodie, I slowly approach the door, cracking it just enough for me to peer through.

Just as Damien has said, their friend is here, standing right outside my bedroom. Somehow, he has made it into the sorority house, up the stairs, and into the dimly lit hallway, even though we always lock the doors. The thought of someone being able to find their way inside makes me feel woozy.

The stranger stands prominently before me, towering over my small frame. He's almost as tall as the doorway. His demeanor radiates safety, yet commands power. He has broad shoulders and a muscular build, his limbs long and well-defined even beneath his clothing. To my surprise, most of his facial features resemble Damien in a way. Dark wavy hair, eccentric blue eyes, a chiseled jawline.

"Quinn?" Jensen questions, on high alert.

"Yeah, I'm here," I quietly mutter. "Your friend is here, too."

"Are you hurt?" Asher asks me, and even though this is the first time I'm hearing his voice in person, there's a noticeable tightness in his tone, too.

All four of them are stressing me out.

"Shhh!" I quickly peek my head out into the dark hallway to ensure we're alone before grabbing his forearm and yanking him into my room.

Once I shut the door behind him, I study him carefully, noticing the perspiration on his forehead. His posture is rigid as he stands motionless in the center of the room. His brows are furrowed, and he doesn't even bother to hide the troubled expression that has claimed his face.

"Asher?" I ask.

"Yeah, that's me," he replies, his voice strained. "Are you okay?"

"Why are you here?"

He blinks at me, mouth agape.

"Quinn," Damien says through the receiver.

"Just happened to be hanging around outside my sorority?"

"I was in the area."

"Right. That's convenient."

Asher avoids direct eye contact and makes his way to my window, peering outside and scanning the surroundings. Suddenly, his gaze becomes fixed on something, his eyes growing wide.

"Damien," Asher warns, raising his voice.

I step beside him, following his stare. My phone falls from my hand and clashes on the hardwood floor as I take in the sight of three tall dark figures standing on the grass below. As if it's not creepy enough being watched by strangers through my window, their faces are hidden by black, beaked masks, illuminated faintly by the moonlight.

Crows.

Is this what they were warning me about?

Am I going to go missing next?

Not only can I not catch my breath, but I've become paralyzed, my bare feet glued to the floor. My knees grow weak and my stomach churns. Whoever these people are, they are staring straight at me, and no matter how hard I try, I can't seem to look away.

"Asher?"

"Quinn?"

"What is it?" Micah demands.

"Fucking talk to us, Asher," Damien commands.

Asher places himself in front of me and blocks me from their view. I back away, not even bothering to retrieve my phone. Asher picks it up instead, takes it off speaker, and sets it against his ear.

"It's them. They're here," he announces. Millions of questions race through my mind. "Yeah, I've got her. She's safe."

"W-who are they?" I rush out while sinking into bed, unable to shake the uneasiness that has swallowed me whole.

Asher ignores me. "They're heading east."

"What is going on? Who are they? Is this another prank?"

"They're out of my view now. We'll be fine. Just go find them." He ends the call and finally meets my frightened eyes. "Do you need to pack a bag or anything?"

BLOODBATH

I shake my head.

"You sure?"

"Everything I need is already at their place," I tell him, visibly shaking at this point. I just can't wrap my head around everything that's happened within the last half an hour or so. I shouldn't have been so stupid, especially after knowing someone was watching me earlier on campus. Why did I brush it off so easily?

Naïve little Quinn, I scold myself.

He sits beside me on the bed, his eyes searching mine. It takes him a while before he breaks the eerie stillness between us. Asher considers what he's going to say next, a cautious look in his eyes.

"Everything's fine," he says bleakly. "It's just another prank."

I want to believe him. I really do.

Although, my gut is telling me that there's something far more sinister going on in the town of Salem, and that I might be next.

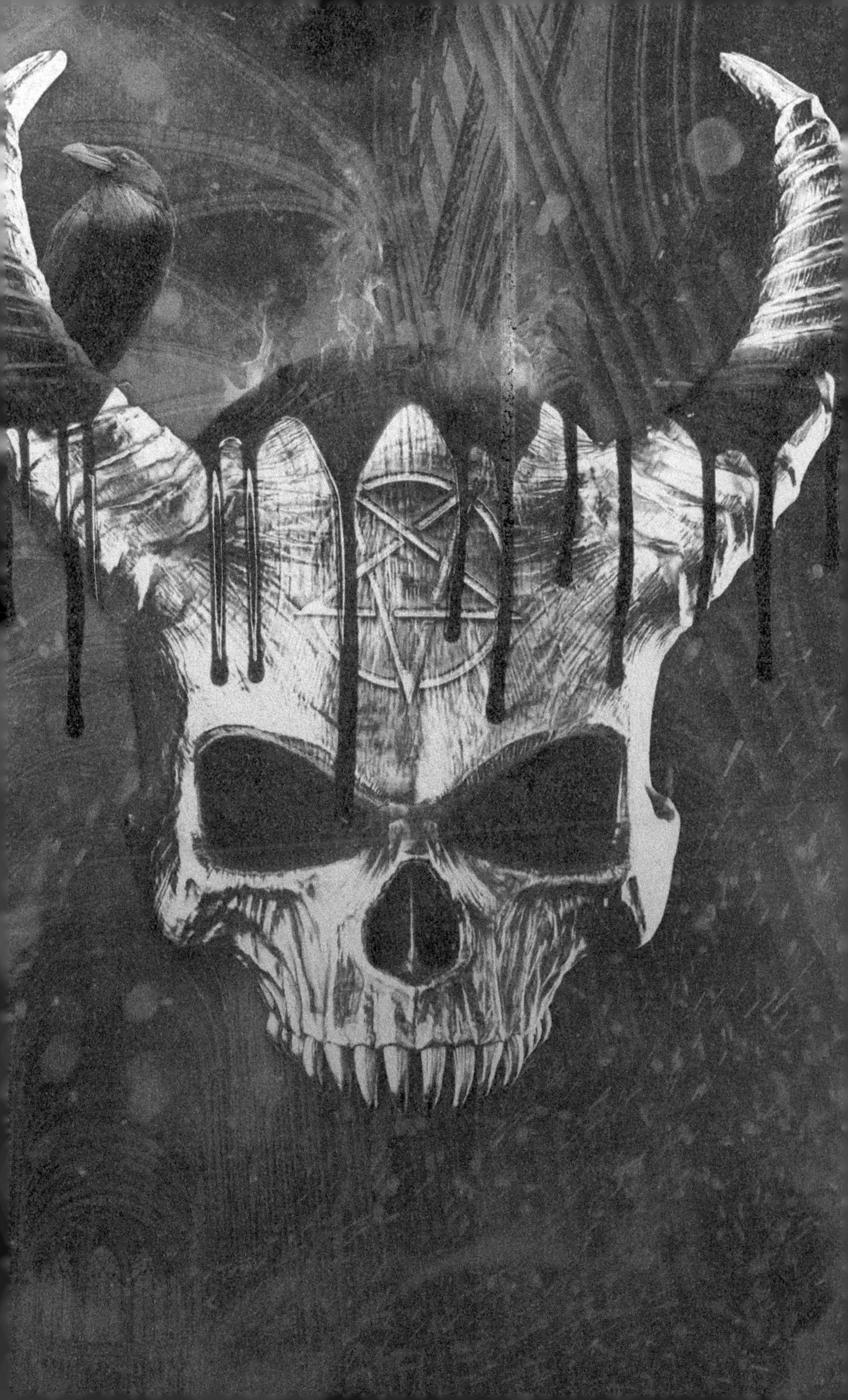

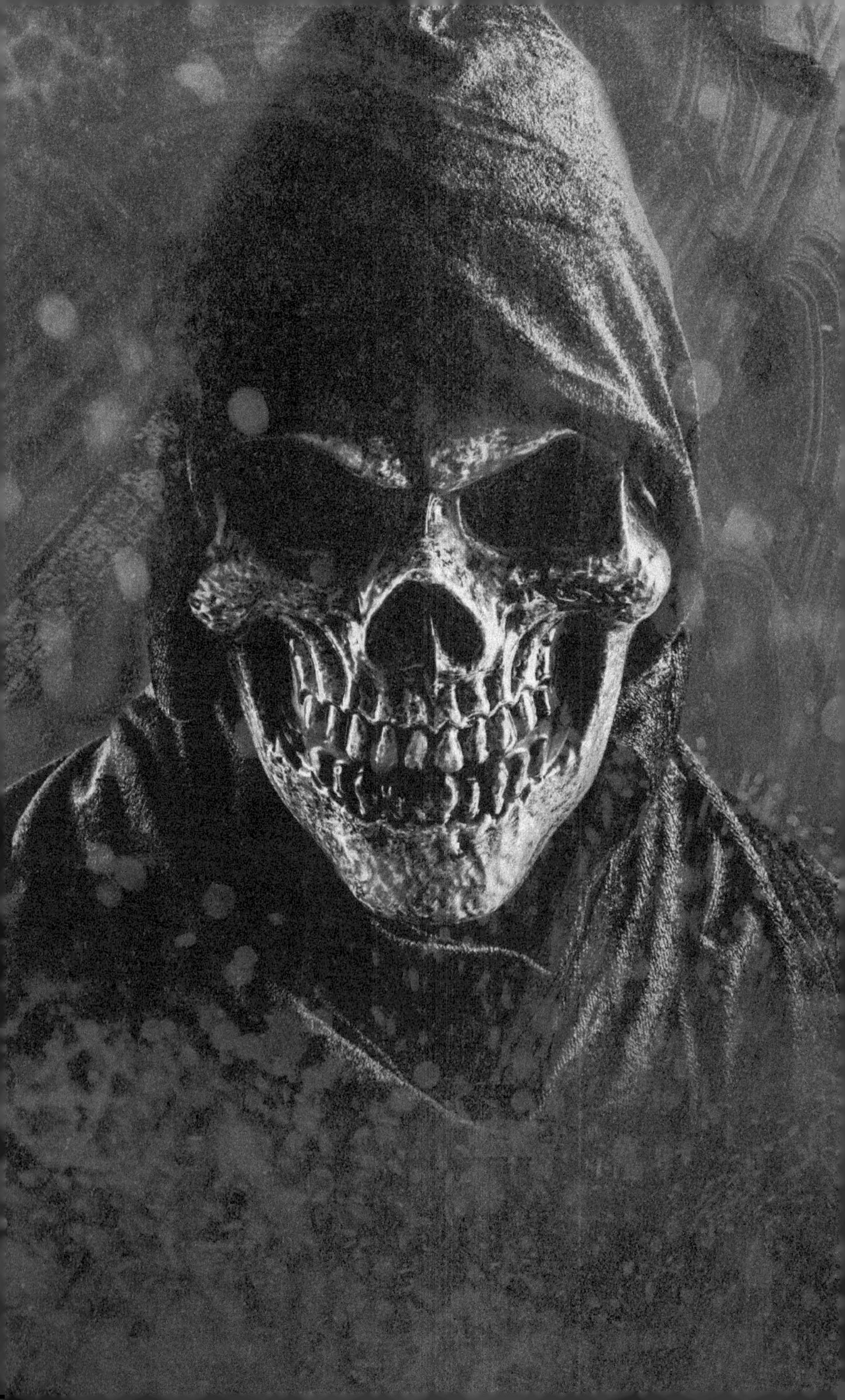

CHAPTER 7

DAMIEN

Jensen floors it down the dark, deserted road, gripping the steering wheel with both hands so tightly his knuckles turn white. "They must be taunting us. It's too soon for them to take her."

"*Try...* to take her," I correct.

"They're acting reckless," Micah blurts out. "They've already taken two girls."

"They might not be dead yet."

"*Yet,*" I emphasize.

"Did you tell him?"

"No..." Jensen says, his voice trailing off.

I turn back to glare at Micah impatiently. "Tell me what?" His face hardens. "Spit it the fuck out!"

"The second girl to go missing," he begins, his shoulders stiffening with each word, "she lived in the house. With her parents."

"The house?"

"*The house*, Damien," he snaps, staring into my eyes.

Letting out a shallow breath, I shut my eyes.

The suicide house on Elm Street.

The house I lived in growing up. The same house I held my mother in when she died in my arms.

That evil piece of shit.

"When did you plan on telling me this?"

"I was waiting for the right time." He plants a hand on my shoulder before I shrug him away. "Quinn and I were driving by on our way back from dinner. The cops were parked out front and speaking with the parents—"

"Quinn," I interrupt. "Did you tell her?"

"Tell her what? About the missing girls?" Gritting my teeth, I shake my head. "About the house? The fuck?" he snaps, defensively. "Jesus, no. Of course not. I would never tell her about that. That's all you. I can't believe you'd even ask me that."

"Well, I don't fucking know," I snap. "I was just making sure."

"You should know me better than that."

"Relax," Jensen orders sharply, raising his voice, the vein in his forehead pulsating. "Now isn't the fucking time. We have bigger issues right now, like finding these sick pricks before they have the chance to take another girl. Especially ours. The first girl went missing from the location where you grabbed your first victim all those years ago. Now this girl is taken from the house you grew up in."

"This can't be a coincidence," Micah says. "They're trying to send a message. They're taunting us, Damien. They're taunting *you*."

My vision becomes clouded, my thoughts in shambles. I can feel myself drifting, consumed with rage and disgust. Doing what Micah has taught me in the past, I focus on my breathing, taking slow, deep breaths as I redirect my attention from Micah's puppy dog eyes and out the windshield instead.

Jensen is right. Fighting right now won't solve anything, and with a deep rage burning in my chest, I can't afford to lose control.

Not right now.

My little Quinn needs me.

She needs all of us.

Suddenly, there's a knot in my stomach.

"There!" I shout, pointing toward Salem Public Library, only about a mile down the street from Quinn's sorority house.

It's them.

I can feel it in my bones.

Three figures dressed in dark cloaks slip into the shadows, vanishing from our sight. I throw open the passenger side door and leap into the bitter air before the Jeep even has the chance to come to a stop. When it screeches to a halt, I briefly hear Jensen and Micah calling out for me to wait, to stay with them, except I'm already one with the darkness.

Although most people fear the absence of light, I welcome it. I find solace in a total black out. It was once the only companion I had back when I slept on park benches and stalked my father's victims.

Over time, I've grown to find tranquility amongst the impenetrable shadows. I gauge my surroundings as I truck through the bushes and trees that lead toward the back of the

BLOODBATH

building.

Every sound becomes more pronounced as I pull my society mask on. An owl hoots from somewhere above me. The dead leaves and ice crunch beneath my boots with each deliberate step I take. I make eye contact with a deer looming in the near distance. The smoke from a fire ignites my senses as I creep further into the night, when suddenly I get a vague scent of copper.

Blood.

I can't tell if it's real, or if I just crave it.

Somewhere to the right of me, a tree branch snaps. I rush toward the sound. Finally, my eyes begin to adapt to the darkness, and out of my peripheral vision I detect movement.

Caww. Caww.

A crow flies past me.

The back door to the library has been left open.

An unsettling silence greets me as I make my way through the wooden doors. The air is still, and what once was a welcoming space has now become a home to evil. My mind begins to play tricks on me, the shadows taking on a life of their own. The floorboards creak beneath my boots with each step as I walk down the narrow aisles, my body on high alert, ready for the inevitable.

Beads of sweat drip down my temples, the towering shelves looming over me as I scan the area for the Hallowed Divine's location, but it's quiet. There's no evidence that anyone is here with me, other than the books watching me from their positions, the spines whispering ominous threats.

Quickening my pace, I turn the corner, frantically searching for anyone I can get my hands on. It's much darker in this aisle, the flickering lamp residing on a table now hidden from another row of tall shelves.

There's a subtle creak from close behind me.

Even with his attempt to catch me off guard, I spin around fast, grabbing hold of the dark figure who managed to sneak up on me. I'm too quick for him. The fucker should have known better. His back collides with the shelf as I slam him into it, books toppling onto the floor beside us. Extending out my arms, I curl my hands around his throat, pressing down.

The crow mask he's wearing confirms our suspicions.

It's them.

The Hallowed Divine.

Realization hits me like a freight train. They've already started their ritual for her. Completely enraged, I begin choking the life out of him, crushing his windpipe beneath my hands. He struggles against my grip, kicking out his legs and swatting at me. He digs his fingernails into my skin. She is mine. Adrenaline surges through me. Mine.

Quinn is mine.

Someone peels me away from him, and when I come face to face with another crow mask, my cortisol levels spike. Lunging forward, I deliver a crushing blow to his abdomen, sending him to his knees. He gasps for air, hunched over in distress.

The other one tackles me from behind, his elbow snug against my throat, cutting off my air. I try to break free from his chokehold by leaning forward, but for the first time in my life, my height puts me at a disadvantage. How the hell is this piece of shit taller than I am?

I grapple with him, throwing us backward and slamming his back into the shelves again and again. He grunts loudly with each impact, and finally, his grip on me begins to loosen.

The guy on his knees stumbles to his feet, leaping toward me. I give him one brutal kick to his chest, sending him hurtling into the bookshelf adjacent to us. Everything becomes a blur. In this moment, I only see red.

BLOODBATH

They got too close.

The guy choking me grows weak, and his arm starts to slip. I reach behind me and peel the mask off his face, clawing at his eyes. He screams, retreating, but I turn fast on my heel, my fist colliding with his nose, then his jaw, the force disorienting him more with each blow.

Fuck.

I wasn't there to protect her.

I grab him by the collar of his cloak and toss him onto the ground beside his buddy, but to his dismay, his friend has somehow managed to escape, leaving this scumbag to me. His swollen eyes are filled with unprecedented terror as he succumbs to my vicious attack.

They're trying to take another woman I love away from me.

"You were watching her?" I question coldly, spitting in his face. "You've been watching *my* girl?"

I continue to beat him until his face is left unrecognizable, and only then do I pull out my knife and press the tip of the blade into his already bloodied flesh. He's barely alert, but thankfully, he's still conscious enough to feel every slice as I carve out his eyes until he's left with empty, hollow sockets.

His pleading and tortured cries are music to my ears.

His sight has now been taken from him. He'll never look at her again.

More anger erupts deep in my chest, and I begin to choke the life out of him, my own blood from my split lip and eyebrow trickling onto him and mingling with his.

A low gurgling sound escapes him.

Red.

I crush his windpipe beneath my hands. He stops struggling, his limbs lifelessly falling to the floor beside his head.

My gaze flickers to the crow mask resting beside the shelf.

Red. Red.
Total black.

JENSEN

"No," I shout when we finally locate Damien. "No, Damien! Stop!"

Micah and I grab hold of his jacket with tight fists, pulling him off and dragging him away.

"You fucking idiot!" Micah scolds, rushing toward the limp, mutilated body on the floor, hoping there's still a bit of life in him.

After a few seconds of silence, he looks up at me with defeated eyes.

"No pulse," he says.

"There was another one. He escaped," Damien explains with a dry tone and blank stare.

"Jesus Christ," Micah snarls.

"This was not the place to shed blood. Not at a fucking school library. You know how long this is going to take to clean this mess up?" Examining the scene before me, the excessive amount of blood along with his crushed facial features, my blood runs cold. We really needed this fucker alive in order to get information on the cult's whereabouts. "What the hell were you thinking, man?"

Spinning on my heel, I turn to glare at Damien, except he's no longer there.

"Shit," Micah curses, scanning the area erratically.

BLOODBATH

"I'll find him." I walk around the pools of blood and make my way down the aisle, following the trail of bloody footprints left by Damien.

The hairs rise on the back of my neck as I look up and down the aisles, following the crimson prints that lead straight to the back door, but disappear once they reach the dirt. I can't find any sign of him. I even check outside around the side of the building, scanning the surrounding area to the best of my abilities. It's quiet for the most part, other than the rustling of dead leaves and the faint sound of the wind. Damien is nowhere in sight.

I make my way back to Micah in defeat. "He got away."

"Fuck," Micah bites out. "He knew we needed him alive."

Kneeling, I double check for a pulse... just to be sure. Nothing.

The moonlight casts a dim glow through the nearest window so we're able to see a bit clearer. "Do you think he blacked out?" I ask, meeting Micah's worried eyes.

He adjusts his mask. "If he did, then we're fucked. You remember what happened last time."

"I'll call Asher," I say, pulling out my phone.

He answers after one ring. "We just got to your place. Quinn is safe. Apollo is here, too."

Letting out a relieved breath, I shut my eyes, pinching the bridge of my nose between my fingers. At least the twins are with her. That's good.

"Can she hear me right now?" I ask.

"She's in the other room. Talk to me. Did you find them?"

"There's a body," I let out grimly.

"Fuck. Who?" Apollo chimes in.

Micah shines the light of his phone onto the face of someone we've never seen before.

"Not sure."

"From the mask here beside him, he's gotta be a member of the Hallowed Divine." Micah snatches the phone from my grasp and places it on speaker. "He was already dead by the time we found him."

"Where's Damien?" Asher inquires. After a moment of silence, he lets out a breath, jumping straight back to business. "Fuck. I'll fill Killian in."

"Good."

"You think we could somehow pull him out of it?" Apollo asks.

"No. He's too unstable right now. Volatile. Don't go anywhere near him. Make that very clear."

"Got it," Asher replies. "Last time he disappeared it was only for two days, right?"

"Yeah, but it can last up to a week depending on his trigger."

"In the meantime, we'll follow behind him and clean up the trail of bodies," Micah declares.

"Has anything come through the police scanner?" I question, crossing my fingers that the answer is *no*.

"Nothing yet," Apollo replies. In response, I release a sharp, thankful breath. "Liam has been listening in since the disappearances of the girls. I told him to report back if anything comes up."

"Last time Damien was triggered, it almost got him killed," Micah lets out warily. " I'll follow him so he doesn't get hurt. He doesn't know what he's doing."

"He's been spiraling for the last few weeks," I point out. "We need to get rid of this body. With all this blood, it's going to take a while to get rid of the evidence. We need to check for security cameras, too."

"Go find him," Asher orders. "We'll send a few guys there to start the clean up on this one."

"I'll call Marcus," Micah offers.

"I got it," Apollo confirms. "Good thing we have him on speed dial and he doesn't sleep."

"Put her on the phone," I tell him.

About a minute later, Quinn's voice is like music to my ears. "Are you guys okay?" she demands, her voice shaky and unsettled.

"We're okay, baby," Micah coos. "How are you holding up?"

"Are you alright?" I ask her.

"I'm fine," she softly replies. "I feel better now that I'm hearing your voices. When will you be here? I'm so creeped out."

"We're so sorry, Quinn," I tell her wholeheartedly. "This has been one hell of a night."

"Why are your friends watching me? This is so weird."

"We just want to make sure you're alright since we're not there."

"Well... hurry back?"

"We have to take care of something really quick," Micah tells her carefully, "but then we should be home. Okay, love?"

"Alright. And Damien?" she questions. "I haven't heard his voice yet." We both look at each other. It's clear the both of us aren't sure how the hell we're supposed to respond. "Is he not with you?"

Micah's lips part as if he's about to answer truthfully, but I cut him off.

"You know how he is," I tell her, trying to make light of the situation. "He's out looking for the fuckers that scared you."

"He's not answering his phone when I call. That's not like him. I'm worried."

"Baby, listen to me," I let out, trying my best to ease her fears. "You're safe. That's all that matters. Everything is going to be okay."

"Hurry back."

"We will," I confirm.

"Jensen?" she urges, her voice trailing off. "I may have been naïve when you first met me, but I'm not anymore. I know there's something you guys aren't telling me. I don't know why you're keeping stuff from me, but that needs to change. It's *going* to change."

Micah lowers his gaze to the ground, consumed with remorse.

Through the guilt, I can't help the grin that claims my face. She's grown so much, and she's so damn smart. I'm so proud of the woman she is. "I know, baby. You're right."

"Please be safe. All of you. It's not just my safety that matters."

My heart twinges. I really hate lying to her, and even though the three of us have decided it's finally time to tell her the truth, telling her at this moment would not be the right call.

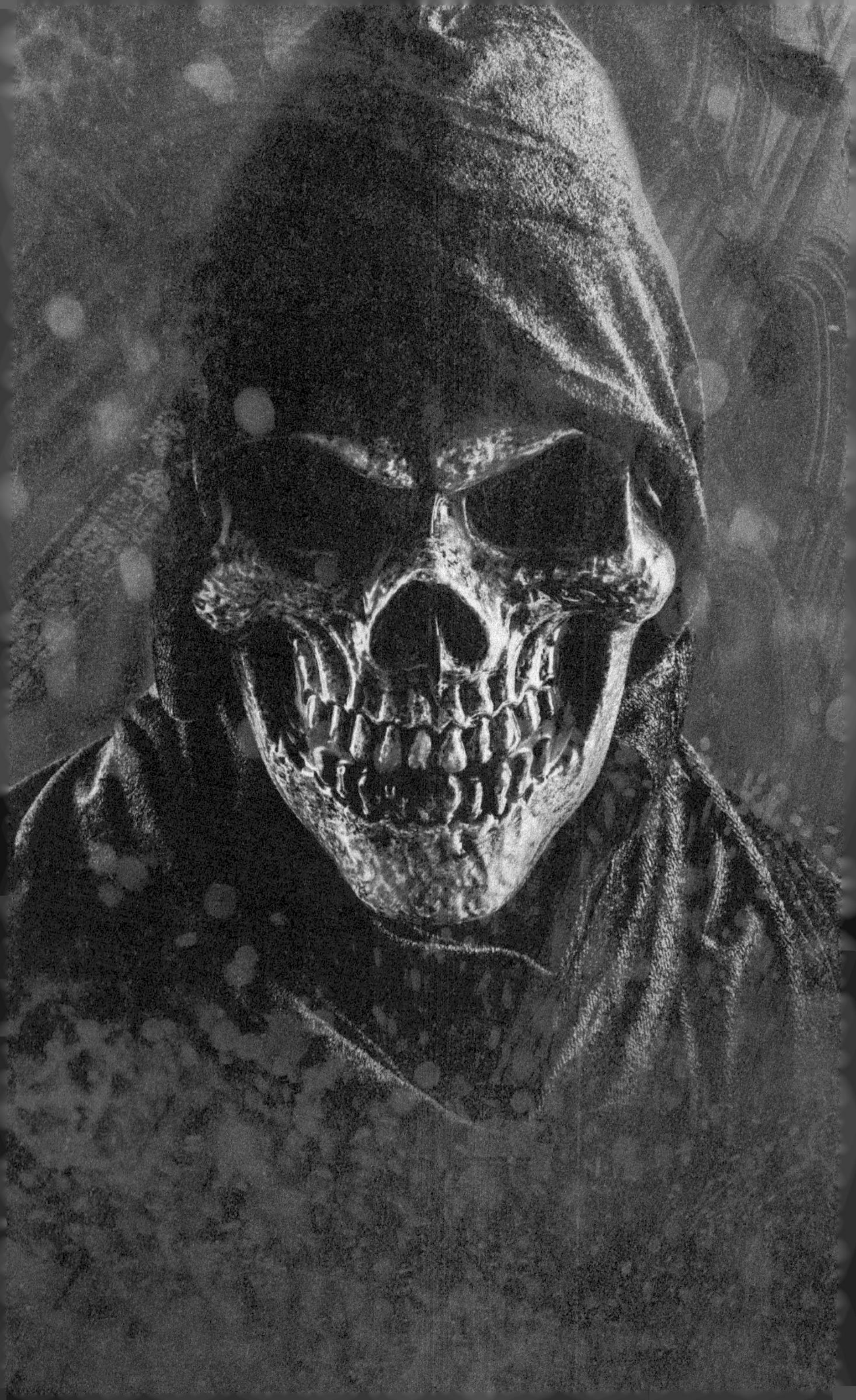

CHAPTER 8

DAMIEN

There's a brutal chill in the air, but my hands are warm. With each blow, his skin splits open beneath my knuckles, painting them red. He deserves to feel real pain. The kind of pain that cannot be described. He likes to beat women. I like to beat men who beat women.

His face transforms before me, his facial features contorting until he's a spitting image of my father. I make sure to stare into his eyes as I toss him into the brick wall and beat the life out of him.

Again. Again. Again. Again.

The shadows are watching. Whispering.

BLOODBATH

I can hear them as I dig into his chest cavity with a blade.
"I'm going to save her," I mutter.
I'm the last thing he will ever see or hear.
Torment is the last he will ever feel.

JENSEN

    The alley is dark, even with the dim streetlight's proximity. The altercation has already broken out. Damien delivers a powerful blow to the man's jaw, using enough force behind his strike that it leaves his knuckles bloody. It's like watching a wolf greedily stalking its prey. His victim staggers backwards with a low groan, his face contorted, and blood spurts from his face with the next blow. He falls backward, his back colliding with the graffiti-covered brick wall. Damien continues his vicious attack, even though it's obvious he has already won.
    It isn't a fair fight at this point.
    I mentally scold myself when my boot meets the shattered glass on the pavement, nearly giving away our presence. Micah grabs my bicep, keeping me from edging closer. The wind blows, which results in the rusted fire escape creaking from over our shoulder. Damien suddenly turns his head in our direction, peering into the darkness we reside in for any potential threats.
    The both of us freeze, chests constricting and shoulders tense. He looks away, unphased, and directs his attention back to the barely conscious man before him. There's an eerie crunch as his fist collides with his nose, along with faint

whimpering.

Damien doesn't show any signs of easing up. He unleashes every bit of his anger. It's hard to watch, especially knowing we can't do anything to stop it. Doing so would only escalate the situation, and that's something we need to avoid at all costs.

With the mindset he's in currently, he's operating way out of character. The usual calm and collected Damien is lost in the dark corridors of his mind. He's frantic and uncontrolled.

We're here for two reasons.

Starting clean up duty until Marcus gets here and ensuring we do everything in our power to keep our friend from getting caught.

For a split second there's a glint of a blade that catches in the moonlight. He steps into him, burying the steel deep into the man's abdomen. We watch as Damien surveys the pain in his victim's eyes, twisting it savagely.

He mumbles something I'm not able to make out. Although he's far from human when he's off the rails, he still manages to keep some of his smarts. He typically goes after the men who are on the Order's watch list for specific reasons. Damien still has some of his morals. Only takes the lives of people who truly deserve it.

But when he gets like this, he's sloppy. He no longer has the ability to see the bigger picture, which can create problems for the society. Even though he makes sure there's a lack of witnesses, at the end of the day, just one thing that slips through the cracks can put us all at risk.

Micah and I continue to maintain a safe distance. Damien withdraws the knife and steps back, allowing the man to slump onto the ground. He wipes the blood off the blade with the sleeve of his jacket and begins to walk away, until the man lets out a low gurgle, spitting out blood.

BLOODBATH

Damien stops dead in his tracks. He pounces on him within seconds, the knife slashing through the air and coming down hard, breaking through his chest. There's so much blood. I lose count of how many times he stabs the guy, carving his carcass like a pumpkin until there's not a shred of life left.

Micah turns away.

With a heaving chest, Damien stands, looking down at him with not even the faintest bit of remorse. He loosens his shoulders and cracks his neck, slipping the bloodied knife into the sheath in the back of his pants. There's an echo from his footsteps as he walks down the desolate alley and eventually vanishes from our sight.

There's an unnerving silence between the two of us. Out of all the brutal attacks we've witnessed, this one was unsettling.

"Come on," I instruct, clearing my throat.

After ensuring we're alone, we head toward the body. My saliva thickens as we examine the aftermath. The gore involved with this one is heavy.

Micah turns his back to the gruesome scene before us, his stomach contents spilling out of him violently. Seeing how distraught he is, kneeling over and wrenching in disgust, I gather his hair in my hand and hold it back for him.

"I'm—fine—" he chokes out. "His dad really fucked him up, man. I—I just want him to be okay—"

"He'll be okay," I assure him, collecting several loose strands and brushing them away from his face.

"I'm sorry," he murmurs.

"You're good, man. Just let it out."

"Fuck," he groans, turning to look at me, his eyes filled with anguish. "Want a kiss?"

"You know I do."

"Gross," he shoots back. "Pretty sure I still have vomit in my mouth."

"I'd kiss you no matter what. Puke and all."

He chuckles, his lips curling into a gentle grin. Given our situation, at least I somehow managed to get a laugh out of him. The space around us becomes quiet, and his face softens, raw emotion erupting within his eyes.

He stares at me with such admiration it leaves me weak in the knees. Love isn't only found in passing stares, forehead kisses or gentle touches. Love is also found in abandoned alleys with rotting garbage and dead bodies. Even with Damien blacked out and causing havoc, the Hallowed Divine's return, and everything important in our life at stake, all of that somehow falls away.

There's a subtle shift in the way he's looking at me. He must know I love him. I think a part of him has *always* known since we were kids.

"Let's get to cleaning so our dumbass friend doesn't get too far," he instructs. "Good thing we have his phone tracked."

"Right."

He shoves his phone back in his pocket. "Dropped Marcus our location."

"Good."

"You should go, Jensen. Step in for Damien." I blink. "I have it from here. I got this."

"You sure?" I ask.

"I'm sure." While stuffing what remains of the dead guy into garbage bags, our eyes meet. "He'll be okay, right?" he asks, looking for reassurance.

"We're a team. We got him."

"We got him," he repeats.

BLOODBATH

DAMIEN

Next on my list: Gavin Sampson.

With a firm grip on the back of his head, I smash his face into the brick wall. Feeling high from hearing the muffled groans of pain that escapes him, I do it again, slamming his face into the building over and over.

I lose count.

Seven?

Twelve?

By the time I drag him backward, his teeth are chipped and he's gurgling, spitting out a mouthful of blood. It gets on my boot.

Irritated, I release my hold on him.

He staggers forward, disoriented, his knees buckling and hitting the pavement. I circle him, watching as he lifts his hand to the gaping wound in his forehead, observing the dark red substance on his fingertips. It drips down his eyebrow and into his eye, painting the white of his eye crimson.

There's a glint from an empty bottle on the ground beside the dumpster. I pick it up and then smash it over his head, glass shattering. I bury the jagged edges into his badly beaten face. I wish his victims were here to witness this, but he doesn't scream like I expected. Instead, it sounds like he's an injured animal, whimpering, cowering... I yank the broken bottle out from his flesh, fascinated with the way the blood spurts in different directions, like a sprinkler.

I do it again.

And then I do it some more.

Until his face looks like it's been put through a blender, skin torn and raw, hanging off by a thread. I'm out of breath. My arms have grown heavy and my fingers are drenched in his blood.

Or maybe it's mine.

MICAH

The days have become a blur.

I can't remember the last time I slept. But I'm not tired.

I'm running on pure adrenaline at this point.

No matter how many guys Jensen sends to tap me out, to give me even just a small respite, I can't pull myself away.

My only thoughts consist of vile images of the brutal murders my best friend has committed.

The only voices in my head are the screams of those he has slaughtered.

I've tried to block them out.

Except... I can't peel my eyes away.

Seeing the person I care about... inflicting so much pain... watching him revel in it... with no end in sight... and not being able to do anything to stop it...

My body feels weaker than it has in years, even with the energy surging through my limbs. My legs grow heavier with each step as I trail close behind him.

By the time we approach the desolated gas station bathroom Zak Sunny has just entered, my head has become

BLOODBATH

groggy.

Damien shoves me against the stone wall behind the bathroom and digs his elbow into my throat, pressing down with so much force I begin to choke. He stares at me with lifeless eyes, his lips in a firm line.

"D-D—Dami—" I croak, clawing at his forearm. "S-stop—"

"Why are you following me?"

I dig my nails into his skin, drawing blood. "I-it's—me—"

"Why the fuck are you following me?"

"D-DAMIEN, STOP—"

Finally, he lowers his arm and steps back. I clutch at my windpipe, fighting through pain, coughing deeply. Knelt over and gasping for oxygen, I look up and meet his eyes.

"It's me," I rasp, one hand cradling my throat and the other on my knee. "I'm—here to help you—"

"Micah."

"Yes?"

"Stay out of my way."

My heart fucking shatters. "Okay," I whisper.

Damien enters the bathroom.

I remain in the cold winter night, just outside the door. I sink onto the ground and fix my gaze on my boots, drowning out the screams until all I hear is a high-pitched ringing in my ears.

I text Jensen again.

He still hasn't answered my last text from earlier today when I asked how Quinn was.

> **Micah**: Too busy for me?
> I'll text her myself.

The ringing in my ears grows louder, causing my vision

to become blurry.
I text Quinn.

> **Micah**: I miss you

> **Quinn**: I miss you, too. Are you okay?

> **Micah**: I'm tired... but okay

> **Quinn**: And Damien? Is he okay? Have you found him?

I want to puke. Pull the hair out of my head. Peel the skin off my face.

> **Micah**: I'm sorry baby

> **Quinn**: I love you, Micah

There's a painful twinge in my chest. Almost as painful as my throat.
Almost.

> **Micah**: I love you, too, Quinn

My ears are still ringing when Damien walks past me, not bothering to even acknowledge my existence. I feel like I'm on the verge of losing it... slowly slipping away, drifting into another dimension.

BLOODBATH

The light flickers as I enter the bathroom. It reeks of cleaning supplies and gasoline. The white tiled floors are sticky with chemicals and bodily substances.

Bleach. Urine. Blood.

So much fucking blood… everywhere…

The poorly painted and graffiti-covered walls… the cracked porcelain sink… splattered across the mirror… dark pools of crimson leading to the very last stall.

He's lying beside the toilet. What's left of his face has been crushed. His nose is flattened like a pancake. His head has also been smashed open, pieces of his skull trailing to where he lays. The stained toilet bowl is filled with brain matter, shattered bones, and teeth.

It looks like soup.

I stare at his body, my chest heaving. Backing away slowly, I pull out my phone, dropping Marcus the location.

Quinn's name pops up on my screen unexpectedly.

> **Quinn**: Please come home

But I can't. Instead, I follow after my friend.

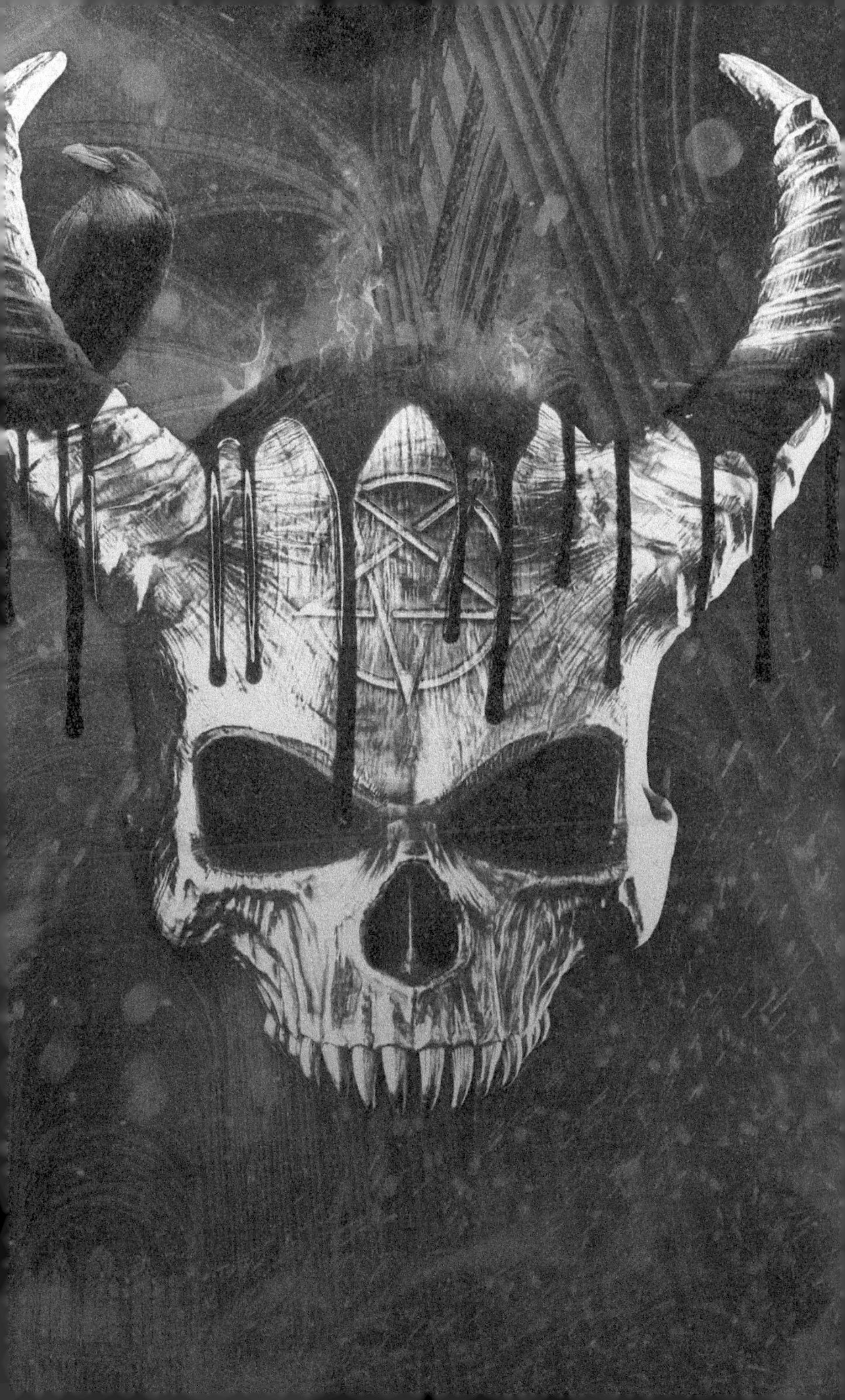

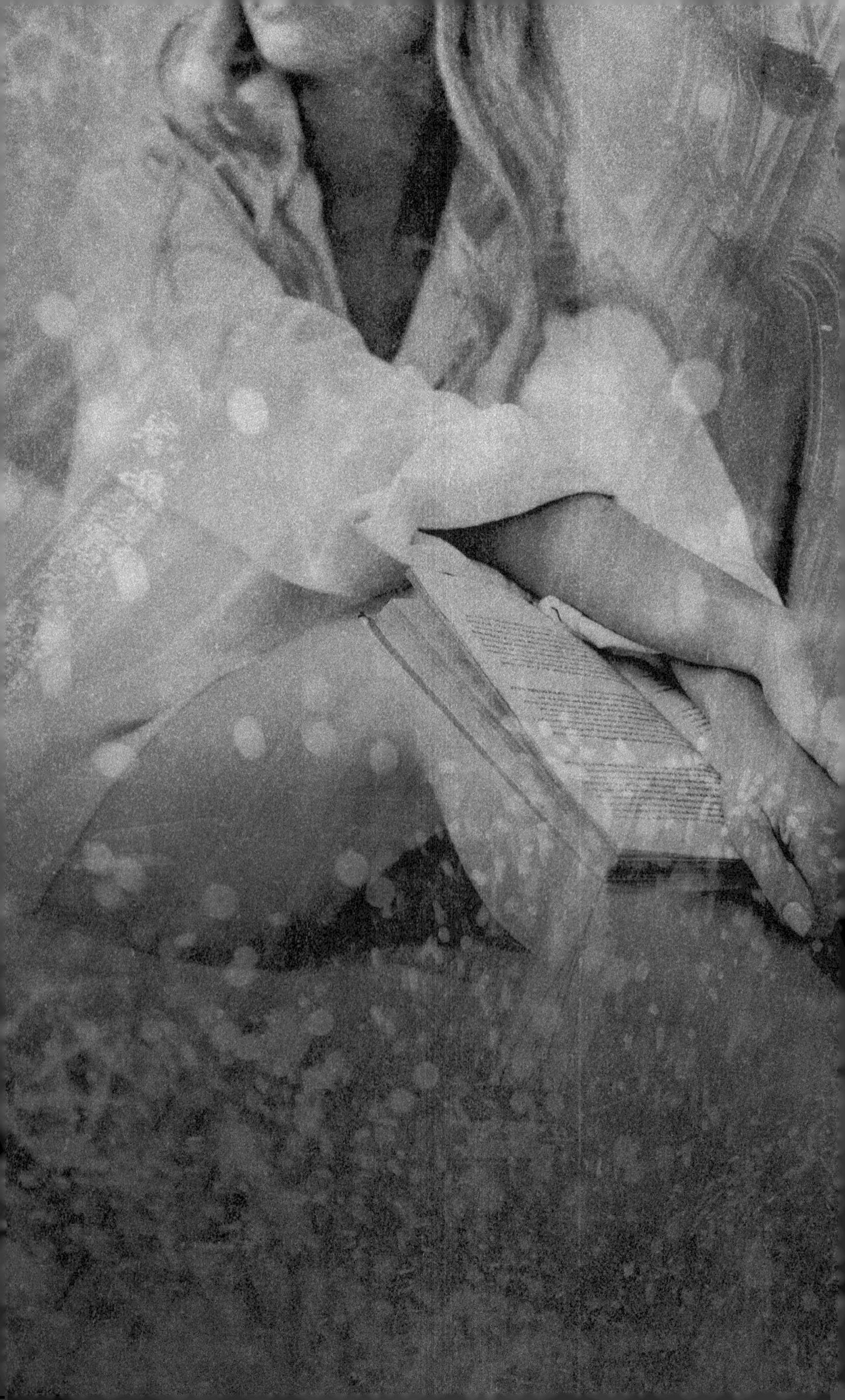

CHAPTER 9

QUINN

THREE DAYS LATER

Clutching the pillow to my chest, I squeeze my eyes shut, cursing my racing thoughts. I just want to sleep. I try to count sheep but that fails to work.

Damn you, sheep.

And damn you, too, sleep.

Damien's been gone for days, but the scent of his cologne still lingers on his bed sheets. I bury my nose into his pillowcase, breathing him in, my stomach in knots. Why won't he come home to me?

The second I roll onto his side of the bed, fighting away

tears, a body crawls into bed beside me.

"Damien?" I question, my eyes lighting up the second I see his mask. "Damien!"

My heart drums wildly as I embrace him tightly.

"Where have you been?"

He cups my breasts with his gloved hands, my nipples puckering beneath the gentle touch of his thumbs. I moan quietly, taking in the blissful sensations of him caressing my body as I stare into the pitch-black eyes. God, I've missed him so much.

His hand grazes down the length of my side, caressing the curve of my hips. I lean in closer, inhaling the scent of his new cologne. It's invigorating, embodying depth and ruggedness.

He grips my ass harshly, causing a soft wince to escape my lips.

"Don't ever leave us again," I whisper, tracing my fingertips along the plastic contours of his mask. He cocks his head to the side, gauging my reaction as he inches closer.

The moment I run my hand down his chest, his body stiffens ever so slightly. My breathing picks up at the sensation of his cold, leather glove caressing my bare skin. I trail my hand further down his chest, resting my palm against his crotch. He grows hard, and I can hear the heavy breath that leaves his lips.

Pulling up the robe he's wearing, I sneak my fingers beneath the hem of his pants, when suddenly, he catches my wrist, keeping me in place. His grip is so tight it's painful.

"Please," I beg, barely any sound to my voice. "I want to *feel* you." I try to break free from his grasp, failing miserably. He clasps his fingers around my wrist even tighter at my attempt, getting a shocked whimper out of me in response. "I *need* to feel you—"

He rolls me onto my other side so I'm facing away from

him. His touch is as light as a feather. He caresses my skin from my shoulder, to my collarbone, to my breasts and downward, his fingertips lingering over the scars on my hip.

Memories come flooding back to me as he traces the initials tenderly, spelling out each letter.

DS.

MH.

JP.

"Please," I breathe softly, spreading my legs eagerly.

His bare hand slips between my thighs, his fingers pushing my panties to the side. I'm so wet, trembling against him as I arch my back, writhing against his touch. He works my clit in slow, precise circles, and the warmth of his touch sends me spiraling. I fight the moans that demand to break free, biting the pillow to silence myself.

But this feels so unbearably good.

It's almost too much.

He teases my entrance, and when he sinks two fingers inside of me, a breathy moan becomes trapped in the back of my throat. He pushes into me again and again, the roughness of his palm rubbing against my swollen flesh, sending shockwaves of pleasure through me.

Oh God, I can feel the orgasm building within me.

He quickens his pace, pumping his fingers into my wetness again and again. I squirm against him, his mask nuzzled in the crook of my neck. The vibrating of my phone against my nightstand takes me by surprise, but I ignore it entirely.

I'm almost there. I'm so close.

"Yes!" I let out a choked sob before his free hand cups my mouth, silencing me.

His demeanor is different tonight; his touch is aggressive. As soon as my inner walls begin to spasm around his fingers, he becomes still, toying with me. I grind myself against his hand, demanding more, and although he's no longer thrusting, the feeling of his fingers curling this deep inside of me tips me over the edge.

I come intensely, biting down on his gloved hand, drooling, shaking, and breathing hard. He pushes his crotch against my ass, his large erection reminding me of how badly he craves me. Only then does he pick up where he left off, working his fingers inside of me, stroking my walls in all the right places. I see stars behind my eyelids, my body tingling as another wave of my climax rushes toward me. I explode around him, grinding my clit against his palm.

My phone vibrates again.

And again.

But I'm unable to move. I've become completely overtaken with exhaustion. Relief.

When I finally catch my breath, and come down from the best high I've felt in a while, he releases me. Lowering his hand from my mouth and removing his hand from between my legs, he pulls away without warning. He stands, fixing his gaze on me as I stare up at him fearfully.

"Wait," I rush out, completely flustered. It's too dark in here. I can no longer see his face. "Are you leaving?"

The vibration from my nightstand distracts me once more. Growling out in annoyance, I reach for my phone and my heart immediately drops.

Damien.

When I turn back to the stranger standing at my bedside, a dark realization sets in.

It's the red mask with devil horns.

He lunges onto the bed, his hands reaching for my throat. I scream out in horror.

Suddenly, my cries pull me from my sleep. I'm covered in sweat, my body raging with adrenaline as I stumble back into reality. Early morning light filters through the window, and just like the last few days, this empty bed reminds me of Damien's absence.

Apollo storms into the room, practically tripping, eyes wide. "What's wrong? Are you okay?"

Asher follows in after him, searching the room in a panic.

I sigh. "It was just a nightmare."

The two of them look at me silently, pondering their response. I hug my knees to my chest and gaze out the window, sadness and frustration bubbling inside me. Asher draws the curtains further to the side and rests his palm against the glass.

"Sorry," Apollo says, observing me from the corner of the room. It almost seems like he's nervous to approach me. "My cousin can be a bit... uh... what's the word..."

"Impulsive," Asher finishes for him. "Hotheaded. Unpredictable."

"Yeah. All of the above."

"A liar," I add, nonchalantly. "I appreciate you both looking after me. Really, I do. But why aren't Jensen and Micah here with me? Why have you both been appointed my babysitters?"

"I'd prefer bodyguards, if anything," Asher mumbles, eyeing me.

Forcing a bitter laugh, I crawl out of bed, their gazes fixed on my every movement. "No offense, but I'm really tired of this."

Apollo steps forward, brows furrowed. "Are you going somewhere?"

I stop dead in my tracks to glare at them. "To the bathroom. Is that okay?"

"Listen, Quinn," Asher blurts out, "you have every right to be upset—"

"I know I do. Nobody is telling me anything, at least not

giving me any real answers. I've barely seen or spoken to my boyfriends. They keep telling me Damien is in trouble and they're looking out for him. I get that, but I feel like I'm trapped here. My friends keep asking where I am. Even though I've answered, nobody has seen me. I haven't left this apartment in three days. I'm going crazy."

"It's for good reason," Apollo states.

Asher shoots a hasty glare in his direction.

"Well, your good reason can eat my ass," I tell them, retrieving a clean towel from behind the door and storming into the hallway. "Leave me alone."

They follow closely in my trail, ignoring my request.

"Please stop following me. I'm taking a shower and then I'm going to get ready for the day," I explain before turning to face them. They back up slightly the moment they see the irritation in my eyes. "Oh, are you both going to join me? I doubt Jensen and Micah want you to see me naked."

"Nope," Asher answers without hesitation. "Not interested in getting my ass kicked."

"I'd rather gouge my own eyes out, save them the trouble," Apollo replies sarcastically. "Plus, you're not my type."

Asher smirks at his brother.

"Good. Then go away." I shut the door in his face.

"You can't leave, Quinn," Apollo calls out.

"I'm not a prisoner!" I argue, slamming a closed fist on the door.

The audacity these two have.

Once I'm dressed, I make myself a cup of coffee, only to realize there's no cream or sugar anywhere in the kitchen. Jensen calls while I'm digging through cabinets and drawers.

Even though I'm angry and fed up, I answer immediately. "Do you have cream or sugar hidden anywhere?"

"I don't think so—"

"Did you find him?"

"Not yet—"

"Alright. I'm going to class." I end the call.

His name flashes on my phone once more. I bitch button him after the second ring and decide to text the group chat I have with my sorority sisters instead.

"I can run to Dunks," Asher offers.

"I'm going to meet a friend at the coffee shop on campus, actually," I reply with a smug grin. "Again, I appreciate you looking out for me, but I can take care of myself now."

"Okay. We'll come with."

"No, thanks. I'll take it from here," I say, grabbing my bag and heading toward the front door, only to find Apollo already in position and waiting for me outside. "What the hell?"

"Where to?" he questions, his tone childlike.

"What do you mean where to?" I ask bitterly. "I don't know where *you're* going, but *I'm* going to grab some coffee with a friend."

He nods. "Sounds great. We ran out of sugar."

"I'm aware, Apollo," I mutter with a sigh, walking down the front steps and toward the driveway. He takes slow strides, ensuring he stays close beside me. "What are you doing?"

With a frown, he shrugs. "Getting coffee?"

"I can go alone."

"No need."

"I want to go alone," I reiterate.

Asher unexpectedly appears on the other side of me. "Not happening."

"What in the fuck," I snarl, running my hands through my hair in frustration. "I was planning on walking. I could really use some fresh air. I feel like I'm going crazy."

"Are you sure?" Asher asks. "It's cold as shit outside."

BLOODBATH

My phone vibrates in my jacket pocket.

> **Jenna**: Sure! I'm already here waiting. Hurry up, bitch

"Fine," I groan. "Let's go."

Apollo opens the passenger side door for me and I climb into the Jeep.

Jenna frowns, her gaze on the twins standing just outside the coffee shop, hovering at the front door with squared shoulders and crossed arms, appearing on guard. "Who the hell are they?" she asks.

"Damien's cousins."

"Do they go to school here or something?"

"Nope."

"Then why are they here? Are they waiting for you?"

"You have a lot of questions, and I'm exhausted," I murmur, taking my usual cup of coffee from the barista with an appreciative smile. "Thank you."

"No problem."

"Woke up on the wrong side of the bed this morning?" Jenna inquires as we sit down at a booth towards the back. I'd like to get as far out of their sight as possible. "Oops. Look at me, asking another question."

"It's been a shitty last few days."

"Why haven't you been home at all? We've been worried about you."

"Sorry," I say. "I didn't mean to disappear like that. I've

been texting you all back, though."

"Well, yeah, but someone could easily have been using your phone and pretending to be you or something."

"I told you all about the creepy guys who were looking into my window the other night. It seriously freaked me out."

She nods in understanding. "I get it. I would've been freaked out, too. The frat guys really need to stop playing pranks on us. We're all on edge lately."

"Pranks or not, my boyfriends were just being overly protective."

"Maybe you're next," she casually points out.

Blinking at her, unsure how to even respond to a statement like that, I tightly curl my fingers around my cup.

Her eyes enlarge with panic. "I'm kidding, Quinn," she says swiftly, reaching across the table and placing her hand on mine. "Babe. Come on. You're not next. I know things are scary right now, but I bet it's just a coincidence that two girls went missing at once. I'm sure they'll turn up soon."

"You say the most unhinged shit sometimes."

"You know I have really dark humor. It helps me get through life. I promise I didn't mean to scare you."

"I know, I know," I sigh, rubbing my tired eyes. "God. I'm a mess. I don't mean to be such a nervous wreck. I have so much going on."

"You know you can talk to me, right?"

"I know."

"I mean it." She caresses the back of my hand with her thumb. "I know I'm the crazy bitch in the friend group, but I really do care about you."

"I care about you, too."

"Then talk to me."

The temptation to spill everything is there, however something inside me worries about how she would react if

BLOODBATH

I revealed the truth. Most friends can share things with one another, details of their relationship, both good and bad. But I think it would be challenging for me to tell her my deepest secrets. How could I explain how I feel like I'm being lied to without being judged? Especially considering my own judgment has begun to feel clouded.

I've never been this girl before.

Looking past so many red flags, so easily.

How would I even begin to tell Jenna that the three men she warned me about really do hurt people? I don't think that conversation would go very well, so here I am, left to decipher my own thoughts… alone.

"Thanks, Jenna," I say with a forced grin, drawing my hand back and fidgeting with both hands in my lap. "I'm okay. I'm just being paranoid."

Am I?

Or am I just finally opening my eyes?

"Alright," she sighs with a slight shrug of her shoulders. "If there's anything I can do to help make you feel better, let me know."

Suddenly, it's like a lightbulb turns on in my head.

"This is going to sound weird," I begin.

"Hit me."

"Do you remember the pig's head that was left on our doorstep?" I ask her cautiously.

With an attentive nod, Jenna leans forward. "Yeah?"

"There was a symbol carved into it, wasn't there?"

Her brows furrow. "I don't remember that."

"Come on," I urge. "Just think."

"I mean, maybe? I'm not sure."

"There was. I know there was. I remember noticing how fucking creepy it looked, like whoever it was that left it there carved that specific marking for a *reason*," I tell her firmly. "It has to mean something. That could be important."

"I guess," she mutters, looking at me like I have ten heads. "Or it could be completely unrelated."

"I... think it might have been a pentagram?"

"Possibly."

"I'm almost positive."

She hums quietly, pursing her lips. "Yeah," she eventually agrees. "I think you're right. It did look like a pentagram. But what exactly does this have to do with anything?"

"I'm not sure. At least not yet."

Jenna accompanies me to the library on campus, but to my disbelief, it's locked. Taped to the large wooden doors is a white sheet of paper with the words "temporarily closed."

"Strange," I murmur. "I wonder why."

Two students walking by happen to chime into our conversation. "I guess a few pipes in the ceiling burst," one of them explains. "The place flooded overnight. Should be opening back up tomorrow, hopefully."

"Got it. Thanks," I tell them.

They begin to walk away until the second student quickly faces us once more. "Oh, I almost forgot," they blurt out, retrieving something from their pocket. "I'm supposed to give you this."

I frown.

They hand me a small folded note and walk down the hall.

Once I see what it says, I become frozen.

You're supposed to say who's there

Paranoia creeps up on me as I remember back to finding the note on my pillow. It's the same paper. Same ink. Same handwriting.

"Wait!" I shout, bolting down the hallway and chasing after the student who gave it to me.

They appear startled when I catch up to them, rightfully so, and Jenna does, too.

"Who gave this to you? Where did they go?" I begin to interrogate, almost incoherently. "Can you describe what they looked like? Did they say anything?"

They gawk at me. "Uh," they mumble, staring at me like I'm crazy. "It was some guy. He paid me fifty bucks. It was easy money and I have a ton of student debt from this shithole—"

"What did he look like?" I interrupt, desperate for answers.

"Quinn," Jenna scolds. "Sorry, my friend is going through some stuff right now. She doesn't mean to scare you."

"It's fine," they reply. "Um, he was really tall. Black hair. Oh, yeah. He had, what do they call them, husky eyes?"

"Husky eyes?" I ask.

"Yeah, when they're such a light blue they almost look see through. He had pretty dark lashes. Kind of looked like he was wearing mascara—"

Damien.

"Tons of tattoos," they add in. "I don't know. It was just some guy. I've never met him before. His request seemed innocent enough—"

"So he told you to give this to me specifically?"

"Yup. Even pointed you out."

My body kicks into fight or flight mode as I search the area frantically. "W-what... like, just now?"

They step backward, creating more distance between us. "A few minutes ago."

"Quinn," Jenna says, her voice shaky. "Are you good?"

My heart races. I swallow.

"Can... can I go now, or?"

I continue to scan my surroundings, completely on edge.

"Yes, you can go," Jenna answers for me. "Thanks for your help. Sorry to bother you."

With that, they scurry away.

"Some guy is passing you notes?" she asks suspiciously. "What does it say? You look super freaked out and it's freaking me out."

I slip the note into my pocket and dig out my phone from my purse, searching "pentagram."

"Quinn?" she questions.

"Yeah, I'm listening."

"No. You aren't." She looks over my shoulder. "You're zoomed in on photos of pentagrams. What do pentagrams have to do with anything?"

"It was this one. The one that's upside down."

She grabs my shoulder in a lousy attempt to snap me out of it. "Okay, now you're really starting to worry me."

"This is why I wanted to go to the library," I quickly explain. "Maybe this is all connected—"

"What's connected?"

Giving her an annoyed stare, I bite my tongue. As much as I appreciate having her tag along with me, at this moment, I'd much rather be alone. I need to focus. Damien has disappeared. Jensen and Micah are hiding something from me. For the last few months, I've had the feeling of being watched. Girls have suddenly gone missing.

Three figures were standing outside my window the other night, and I can't help but feel like maybe I'm the center of it all. If nobody else will tell me what the hell is going on, then I need to figure it out myself.

The worrisome expression plastered on my friend's face has me questioning whether or not I'm losing my shit. Yet, deep down, something in my gut is encouraging me to keep digging, no matter what anyone thinks.

"I'll see you later, Jenna," I blurt out, walking quickly in the other direction.

BLOODBATH

"Hey! Where are you going?" she calls out from behind me.

I continue to take long strides over to where Asher and Apollo are waiting. As irritated as I am with the two of them following me all over campus, I approach them with a determined grin.

Apollo sips his coffee.

Asher smirks down at me, cocking his head to the side. "Going to yell at us some more?"

"Nope," I say. "I actually wanted to ask for a favor."

Apollo narrows his eyes.

God, the two of them look so much like Damien. My heart twinges at the thought.

"Can you walk me back to my sorority?"

Asher folds his arms over his chest, looking at me suspiciously. "Don't you have class?"

With a deep breath, I straighten my posture. "I'm ditching."

"That's unlike you," Apollo mumbles.

"How would you know?" I challenge. He shrugs before clearing his throat. "I need my laptop. I have to… study."

"Study," they reply in unison.

"Yes. Study."

"You can't stay there," Apollo states.

"You can take me back to their place after," I reply innocently. "I just need to grab my laptop. Please. It's important."

The twins look at one another before meeting my eyes once more.

"Okay," they say.

After locking myself in Damien's room and hours of research on pentagrams and the missing girls cases, I've come to one conclusion.

I don't have the slightest fucking clue as to what the hell is going on in Salem.

But there's one theory that stands out the most.

There's a cult of killers in this town.

It sounds insane, but it could be the link to everything that's been happening. I get the brief urge to call it into the tip line, but decide not to.

I continue my deep investigation on the internet and go through several forums dedicated to this theory. Apparently, there have been many missing person cases over the years. These instances have several common connections.

Women.

Symbols carved into the head of a pig.

And... a full moon.

MICAH

"Will you answer the goddamn phone, jackass?" I demand, practically shouting into the void since Jensen has also seemed to have disappeared over the last two hours.

The sun has already dipped below the horizon. I pace the empty park beneath the muted lamplight, blowing warm air into my icy hands. Damien's on a bench off in the distance, finally sleeping. Will he sleep it off?

Probably fucking not.

BLOODBATH

It's been a wild last few days and I've barely slept myself. A cold, gentle breeze rustles the dead leaves on the crystalized ground. A tall silhouette comes into my view at the end of the pathway, walking through the empty swing sets and playground.

I know it's Jensen.

Instead of being relieved that he has finally shown up, I catch myself bubbling with anger and resentment.

"Hey," he says quietly once he reaches me.

I glare coldly at him. "Look who finally decided to show up."

"Come on, man," he groans under his breath. "I've had my hands so full. I'm tired."

"Oh, you're tired," I smugly question, spitting on the ground beside his boots. "You're not the only one who is fucking tired, Jensen."

"Don't start."

"Don't start?" I echo, giving him a good shove, watching as he stumbles back, his eyes filling with rage. "Fuck you."

"What the hell is your problem?"

"You have your head so far up Killian's ass, it's pathetic!"

"This is what we agreed to, Micah," he snaps back at me, his lips pressed into a firm straight line. "You're the one that decided on it. That I'd step into Damien's position in the Order while you look after him."

"You're so busy you couldn't answer my call?"

"I was here, getting out of the car," he argues, laughing. "Jesus Christ. You're like a toddler when you don't get your way."

"You've barely talked to me. I've been seeing the most awful fucking shit, things I will never talk about, or think about, things I wouldn't—I couldn't," I stutter anxiously, my heart pounding forcefully in my ribcage, limbs still trembling with left over adrenaline.

He reaches for me, but I jump back, planting my hands on the back of my head in distress.

"Micah, I'm sorry," he says softly. "I didn't realize you were having such a hard time."

"He's finally passed out. You can go now."

"No."

"Just fucking leave. I got this. He's fine. I'm fine. Sorry I called."

"Have you slept at all?"

I snort. "Like you care."

"Damn right I care," he responds angrily, studying my face closely. "That's why I've been sending people to tag you out, but you keep sending them back. You're not letting anyone help you."

"I'm not fucking leaving him." I look over my shoulder and find relief when I confirm Damien is in the same spot.

"You don't have to leave him, but shit, man, shut your eyes for a few minutes here and there. Let us help. Get some rest or you're going to slip up."

"I'm not going to slip up. I have energy."

He arches a brow. "Are you manic right now?"

I'm annoyed at being micromanaged, but I know it just means he cares, "No. I wish I was. I'm running on energy drinks and nicotine. I said I'm fine. Don't act like you suddenly give a shit. You're busy. Go do orderly things."

"Micah," he groans, pulling me into him.

For a second, I give in, my body dissolving against his. My legs feel like Jell-O. My arms feel so goddamn weak. My knees are shaky. Burying my face in the crook of his neck, I breathe him in. My pulse begins to slow its sporadic beating, finding a steady rhythm and calmness I haven't felt in days. We embrace each other closely, soaking in each other's body warmth beneath the twinkling night sky, while our friend rests on a cold, hard bench… struggling.

Battling his inner demons… all on his own.

Pushing Jensen away, I shake my head in denial, the bitter air nipping at my skin.

"I pissed you off, and for that, I'm sorry," he blurts out. "I got caught up in my own shit and haven't been here for you. I'm sorry. I'm fucking sorry. How many times do you want me to say it?"

"You've been real close with Killian, though, haven't you?"

"What?"

"Are you fucking him?"

"Hell no." I swallow. "Wait a second. Is that what this is about?" he accuses, raising his voice. "You're upset I've been spending more time with Killian? You're *jealous*?"

"I don't know what you're talking about," I snap, guarded, as an icy gust of air sweeps through us.

He laughs.

I grimace at him while he does it, taken by surprise.

"Yeah, you do. You know exactly what I'm talking about. I know you like the back of my hand."

I force an unimpressed laugh. "Do you?"

"You're jealous. Jealous, *and* an idiot."

"Oh, fuck you, Jensen," I scoff, pressing a firm finger on his sternum while staring into his eyes furiously. "The other night, I told you how I feel, and if you don't feel the same way, that's fine. Just stop being a coward and fucking tell me."

"You're fucking stupid." He leans into my touch, our faces only inches apart, his breath fanning my lips. "I'm balls deep in love with you. What are you talking about?"

My jaw drops.

"I thought that was really fucking obvious," he continues, his gaze locked with mine, conveying passion and sincerity.

"I thought I didn't have to say it. But here. I'll say it again. I'll scream it into the abyss if you want me to." He aggressively takes my face between his hands. "I love you, dumbass."

Suddenly, my heartbeat quickens.

"Damn you, Peterson," I breathe softly.

He presses his forehead to mine. "Not romantic enough for you?"

"Are you joking? It couldn't get more romantic than this."

His lips curl into a grin.

"I love you, too, Jensen," I declare. "Always have."

"I know, Micah. I feel it. Every day."

I've never heard his tone this soft and tender. The world around us fades into the background as I take in the significance of his words. So simple, yet so powerful.

The *dumbass* just adds a special touch.

Jensen Peterson not only loves fucking me, *but fucking loves me.*

I feel a sense of complete validation. All this time, I think a part of me has always known that he loves me, since we were just two innocent kids lost in the system. But hearing him say it with my own ears has sparked something in my soul.

He places his hands on my chest, his eyes exploring mine. Grabbing the collar of my jacket, he draws me closer, brushing his lips against mine. "It took us how many years to say it out loud?

"I lost count," I say, slamming my mouth against his, holding him passionately beneath the stars.

"Please, go home and sleep," he murmurs into our kiss.

"No."

"Take a shower. You smell like shit."

Wrapping my arms around him tighter, I sigh. "You don't smell so great, either."

"You've been doing a good job."

"I know."

He tilts his head to the side and kisses me deeper, taking in sharp breaths and tangling his hand in my hair. "Will you sleep if I stay with you for a while?"

"Maybe."

He sits down on the nearest bench and looks up at me, almost waiting for me to give him a hard time. I sit beside him for a minute, stubbornly looking up at the night sky as he pulls his winter hat over my head, warming my painfully red ears. I don't even try to argue with him about it. I know it won't do me any good. Even though he's staying with me, I'm reluctant to give rest a real shot, until eventually, I catch his eyes, noticing the frustration within them.

He's exhausted, too.

With an exhale of defeat, I submissively lift my legs onto the bench and lie down, resting my head in his lap.

Within seconds, I'm down for the count.

"Fuck," Jensen curses loudly, moving me from his lap and abruptly pulling me from my sleep.

"W-what?" I stammer, getting reacclimated with my surroundings as I stand.

"He was just there a few minutes ago," he nervously lets out, rushing toward the bench where Damien once resided.

"What the hell happened?"

"I think I dozed off for a minute or two. Jesus fucking Christ. I can't believe I—"

"Hey." I grab him by the shoulders. "We'll find him."

QUINN

The sound of the front door opening is loud in the late hours of the night. If I didn't just get out of the shower twenty minutes ago, I'd probably still be asleep. I wrap my damp hair in a towel and make my way toward the living room, expecting to see Apollo or Asher sitting at the table. However, they're not in their usual spot.

The room is empty.

Maybe it's Jensen or Micah. They've been out searching for Damien for what feels like every minute of the day. I know they promised they would call me the second they find him, but I still can't help but have hope that maybe it's *him*. Even after all the times I got my hopes up only to have them shot right back down.

This whole thing has been absolute torture. I've barely eaten. Barely slept. I'm so exhausted at this point that when Damien steps into my view, I'm sure I must be dreaming.

"Damien?" I whisper.

My heart leaps at the sight of him, especially when my gaze catches the blood splattered on his shirt along with his bruised face. He takes long strides into the kitchen, his heavy boots tracking dirt in his path. When his gaze meets mine, it finally hits me.

This is really happening.

"Damien!" I squeal.

Suddenly, I'm clinging to him, my nails digging into his black leather jacket. Tears spring to my eyes. I hold onto him for dear life, hoping that if I hug him tight enough, he won't be able to slip away again.

He doesn't move. He's as cold as ice and as still as stone. This doesn't feel like him. It feels like someone else entirely. I draw back just enough to look up at him.

"Are you hurt?" I ask, observing the dried blood on his throat and jaw.

Dark bags reside beneath his vacant eyes, his lips pressed into a firm straight line. My breathing quickens along with my pulse.

Asher bursts into the room, eyes wide as if he's seen a ghost.

"He's home," I say, stating the obvious.

But there's this weird look in Asher's eyes. He digs out his phone from his back pocket, watching us carefully.

"Damien?" he questions, his voice tight.

We get no response.

"Damien," I say again, more loudly this time. Frustrated. Angry. "Where the fuck have you been?"

"Around," he lets out, his voice falling flat.

"What the hell is that supposed to mean?"

"Quinn," Asher warns.

"No, Asher! He hasn't answered any of my calls," I press, now glaring at the man I love. "All this shit has been happening to me and you decide to leave me high and dry? Instead of explaining, you disappear? Clearly you know something you're not telling me."

Damien's jaw twitches.

"Take it easy, man," Asher says to him.

"What are you doing?" I ask sharply, confused out of my mind. "Stop being so easy on him. He scared the shit out of us and comes home as if nothing has happened? That's bullshit and you know it!"

"He's not here, Quinn," Asher states, his voice tight.

I take in a deep breath.

"He's blacked out."

"What do you mean he's blacked out?"

Asher steps forward cautiously, his voice calm. "This happens to him sometimes—"

"Don't give me that—"

"Listen to me, Quinn," he stresses. "He's not *here*."

Damien takes slow strides to his room. I trail closely behind him, ignoring and tuning out Asher's words entirely. I step into the center of the room and keep my eyes locked on my boyfriend as he shuts the door with a loud thud. He almost seems annoyed with my questions. When he turns to face me, my heart skips a beat. The usual spark in his eyes has been replaced with a detached, hollow gaze.

A dead stare.

It's as if a light has gone out, like even though he's physically here with me, he's mentally absent.

I didn't realize the seriousness behind their warning until now.

There's a tightness in my stomach. I can feel the blood pulsing in my body. Damien remains perfectly still, staring at me blankly. The emotional distance between us sends shivers down my spine. With squared shoulders, and arms firmly at his sides, he slowly stalks toward me. His features appear carved from stone.

As unsettled as I am, I stand my ground. "Where the fuck were you?"

The heat drains from the room, immediately replaced by a coldness, goosebumps pebbling my skin. With each step forward, his movements seem robotic.

"I called you. Over and over. Why didn't you answer?" I question him, staring up into his eyes.

BLOODBATH

"I was busy," he dismisses.

"That's your excuse?" I bark, gazing up at him in horror. "What was so important that you fell off the grid? Days passed and you couldn't even answer your phone? Not even a simple text?"

His eyes appear unfocused, like even with our intense eye contact, he's staring past me.

"Answer me," I say, desperation coating my tone. "Do you even know who I am right now?"

He abruptly closes in, spinning me around swiftly. My heart drums rapidly as he forcefully pushes my front against the nearest wall, his forearms locking me in. Shocked with his action, I blink through blurred vision, trying to catch my breath.

Pressing his body into me, he replies with a soft, soothing yet ominous voice. "I know *exactly* who you are, princess. You're my whole fucking world."

I have a strong desire to resist him, given that he hasn't come home in days, or even bothered to call, yet the ache between my thighs is relentless. As intimidating as his body language has been, and how careless he seems to be, I can't dismiss how badly I crave him. Especially given the fact I can feel his cock throbbing against me.

"I hate you for scaring me," I say under my breath.

I press my face against the wall along with my trembling hands. He tears off my silk robe, my nipples hardening as the cold air grazes my skin. I can feel him breathing heavily from behind me, ripping off his own clothes.

"What the hell do you think you're doing?"

He lets out a cold laugh, then kicks at my ankle, spreading my legs. "Taking what's mine."

"Fuck you," I hiss.

"You are going to take every inch," he sharply orders, the

tip of his cock teasing my entrance, "while I *gut you* with my cock."

"Fuck you," I repeat, fighting against him, yet craving him desperately.

He overpowers me, slamming into me with passionate aggression. A cry falls from my lips. I don't even have the chance to accommodate his thickness. I can feel him growing harder... bigger.

Fighting through tears, I take him.

"I hate you so much right now," I whimper.

"Do you want to know what I did to them?" he questions, his voice filled with venom.

Something cold and sharp traces along my waist. I wince from the threatening sensation, becoming motionless, scared to make any sudden movements.

"I-is that a knife?" I ask.

"You're so pretty," he replies coolly, grazing the metal tip down my jaw, stopping at the arterial pulse in my throat.

He moves within me, grinding his pelvis against my ass forcefully, burying himself deeper in my core with each stroke.

I call out his name loudly, angrily, my moans bouncing off the walls. He applies slight pressure, pressing the knife into the sensitive skin on my shoulder, drawing a small bead of blood.

"Good girl," he exhales, circling his lips over my shoulder, tasting me on his tongue.

The sting of the cut and the ungodly ache between my legs sends me right into oblivion. He releases a soft groan of satisfaction, dragging the sharp point down my spine, then pressing into my hip, not hard enough to break skin but enough to send my endorphins skyrocketing.

"I cut into them, too," he reveals, the darkness within him

casting a shadow over the room. "I made them suffer."

"Who?"

Suddenly, he slips the tip of the knife between my legs, resting the flat, cold edge of the blade over my clit.

"Careful," he states, pressing down more firmly on my sensitive flesh while sinking into me more slowly. "It's... sharp."

I freeze, unable to clench my thighs without the threat of being cut.

"Damien," I gasp fearfully, my legs trembling.

But the coldness of the steel pressed against the most intimate part of my body sends my endorphins into overdrive.

My heart slams against my ribcage.

When I begin rocking my hips forward, he applies more pressure, the dull edge of the knife grazing along my skin.

I moan softly, sharp, uneven breaths escaping my lips.

"Look at you, grinding your wet pussy on the weapon that claimed the lives of so many worthless, broken men," he groans callously, slamming into me harder, my body jerking forward.

The knife slips ever so slightly.

My eyes shoot open when it registers in my brain.

"Damien," I blurt. "Careful—"

"I fucking tortured them, Quinn," he grits out. "I made them bleed for us. They felt it all. Every... stab... piercing through their flesh. Over and over. They felt it all." He deepens his thrusts, rocking into me with an urgency, slamming his pelvis against my ass while rubbing the flat side of his knife over my clit in slow, circular motions.

I cry out helplessly from his words and actions, both from fascination... and absolute horror.

"I did it for you, Quinn. I do it all... for you."

The tip of the blade breaks skin, a burning sensation

creeping down my thigh.

"Damien," I call out to the man... *I love...* knowing it's him, while also knowing... it's not him. *Not right now.* "Damien..." I breathe sharply, tensing up, terrified to make any sudden movements. "Damien, prove it—"

"Prove it," he echos, a chilling laugh departing his lips.

He pulls out of me swiftly, the loss of contact leaving me on edge. Scared to look back, I remain motionless, sweaty palms and forehead pressed flat against the surface of the wall, my mind and body on heightened alert.

The abrupt groan that leaves his chest next is explosive. It's the kind of pleasure derived by pain. Damien lurches forward, and although I can't see what he's doing, I know his attention is focused between his legs, his hands working in short, sudden movements, matching his exaggerated breaths.

"Oh, fuck," he chokes out.

When I finally find the courage to look back, my stomach sinks. I gasp for air, watching intently as Damien finishes carving the last letter, his cock straining with desire, and now painted red.

He's cut my initials into the tender, most intimate part of his body.

Blood drips from the Q, then the R.

"Oh, oh my—God," I pant, my lips trembling.

As insane as this is, watching Damien display such erratic and unsafe behavior, my stomach flutters. Heart hammers. Breathing quickens, matching his. There's something so fucking erotic about this moment, I can't seem to pull my gaze away, no matter how hard I try.

Positioning himself against my entrance once more, his cock slick with both blood and arousal, he slips back inside me.

That does it.

BLOODBATH

"Ghost," I scream out in bliss.

With his lips beside my ear, he stills.

"Fuck," he mutters, the knife dropping to the floor.

Craning my neck, I meet his eyes, relieved to see the warmth has unexpectedly returned. "Damien?"

"You're... bleeding." He groans at the feeling of my pussy gripping him as he moves within me.

"You are, too..."

"Did I?" he asks, unsure. "Fuck... What—Oh, fuck, you feel so fucking good, I can't think—"

"Where have you been?"

"I'm right here, baby," he whispers, moving his hips against me. "So deep inside you... my favorite place in the whole fucking universe."

"You cut yourself..." With a whimper, I claw at the wall, my nails chipping the paint. "You've... been gone. You disappeared."

When he begins to draw back, I reach behind me, keeping him close.

"I—" He traces his lips along my throat and then kisses the tender spot just below my ear. "—I'm sorry. That happens sometimes."

"Don't fucking stop," I demand, pushing back against him with each thrust, fighting through the discomfort between my legs.

"Fuck, baby, you feel to die for," he whispers, sinking his teeth into the tender skin on my shoulder.

I shudder, my body vibrating with pleasure. "It hurts," I tell him, reaching behind me until my hand cups his firm ass. He sinks into me deeper with slow, sensual strokes. I can feel the blood trickling down my thigh. "I'm so mad at you."

He pulls out of me with a soft exhale, turns me to face him, and sinks to his knees.

"I know," he coos, positioning his face between my legs.

He traces his tongue over the small cuts on the crease of my thigh, licking away the small beads of blood. There's something so erotic about watching him tend to my wounds with his tongue, his eyes locked on mine the entire time as he plants tender kisses on my raw skin. With crimson-colored lips, he works my clit, sucking me into the warmth of his mouth.

He groans loudly, licking up and down my pussy before thrusting his tongue into my hole. Gripping the back of my legs, he shakes his head, nuzzling his nose against my bud roughly. The friction feels so incredible. My thighs burn. My pussy spasms around his tongue, his finger teasing my ass.

But as amazing as this feels, the red hot tension between us thickens in the air.

I pull hard on his hair, guiding his head closer, his face suffocated by my thighs, giving him no room to breathe. His body stiffens as he devours me with his mouth, his thumb sinking into my ass.

While grinding my pussy against his face, my legs begin to give out.

"Get on the fucking bed," I order.

With a sharp intake of air, he obeys. When I push him onto his back, his eyes widen, reflecting a sense of urgency.

"Look what you did to yourself," I demand, the skin between his thighs smeared with blood. He doesn't seem to care.

"Sit on my fucking face," he murmurs, his voice pleading. "Sit on my fucking face, *please*."

I do just that.

My thighs hug his head and I ride him, using his mouth for my own personal gain.

"Shut up," I say, grinding my pussy against the length of

his tongue.

His grip tightens painfully on my thighs, his heavy breathing and groans echoing with mine. I'm so angry I can't stand it, but even with the anger, our passion is undeniable.

His saliva coats my pussy, his bloody tongue ravishing me like I'm his last meal.

"Fuuuuck," he whimpers against my flesh. "You taste so fucking good. Use me, baby. Fucking use me to come."

Just as I'm about to spiral, I pull away.

"Need more—"

"Shut up, Damien." I straddle his hips and lower myself onto him, taking him entirely. "Just shut the fuck up!"

He draws in a soft, stuttering inhalation, staring up at me with a sense of immediate need.

"I missed you," I cry out, pinning his arms beside his head. God, I feel crazy. So many emotions are flowing through me at once, like a flood.

He watches me quietly, his lips parted as heavy groans escape his chest. I focus on his eyes, noticing the remorse behind them. I come down forcefully on his thick cock, glaring down at him with all the anger that has built within me over the last several days.

"I couldn't fucking breathe," I bite out, tears spilling from my eyes and splattering on his chest.

He swallows hard. "I know—"

I release my grip on his wrists and curl them around his throat. "No," I argue over him, bringing myself down harder on his pelvis. "You don't fucking know, Damien, because... you. Weren't. Here."

His face turns red, matching his swollen lips.

"There's a killer in town, and you were gone..."

He screams *I'm so fucking sorry* with his eyes.

"You think using a knife you've killed people with to make

me come... and cutting my initials into your skin will make me forget? Make it all better?"

Damien holds my gaze and takes every bit of resentment and frustration I unleash on him. I straighten my arms, applying more pressure to his throat as I bounce on his shaft like I'm in heat. My head becomes heavy, my neck rolling back until the towel holding my hair unravels, falling somewhere behind me.

"You weren't fucking here," I whimper, my walls clenching around his thickness as I ride him savagely, rocking my hips aggressively, digging my fingers into his skin. "You're all. Fucking. Lying. To. Me."

He groans in disapproval, his eyes glistening beneath the moon light invading the room. "Baby, I— I don't know what happened. I'm... sorry," he croaks.

"I'll leave... I'll fucking leave you."

"No," he grits out, his pupils dilated, brows furrowed. "You wouldn't— you won't."

I slam myself down harder on his shaft, tightening my grip on his throat. "I will."

He grows harder, twitching inside me. "Don't say that. *Please* don't say that."

From built up emotions and the thought of nearly losing him, and with complete euphoria raging through my body, I ease the pressure on his throat. He inhales sharply, his chest rising and falling intensely with each strained breath.

"I hate you."

"But I—"

I lean forward, clinging to him desperately, my forehead pressed against his broad shoulder. He wraps his arms around my back and embraces me through my orgasm.

"Don't leave me." Damien lets out another strangled breath, squeezing the life out of me. "I'm done lying. Please don't leave me." Damien becomes still, releasing sharp, shallow groans as he spills himself inside me. "Please don't fucking leave me. You're my little Quinn, and I'm your Ghost. It's so dark without you. I'll do better— I promise I'll do better," he groans, burying his face in the nape of my neck, stifling his moans.

The door opens abruptly, crashing against the wall. Micah and Jensen both speak simultaneously.

"Quinn..."

With Damien still snug within me, I crane my neck, meeting their gazes.

"Damien?" Micah gasps. "You're... *here*..."

"Yeah," Damien answers.

Jensen approaches us, staring at Damien apprehensively. "You good?"

"I'm fine?" he questions, gesturing down to where we're both still joined with a nod. "I'm better than fine, actually. She's so warm."

"You think this is a fucking joke?" Jensen asks.

"No?"

Micah looks angry. "Quinn," he says quickly, his gaze focused on the smeared blood on our bodies.

"I'm okay. I wanted it."

"We're both fine," Damien responds as we stand. "I don't know what everyone's problem is."

With tilted heads and pursed lips, they stare at him.

Damien's eyes narrow in response. "Dude. What's your fucking issue?"

"*My* issue?" Jensen rubs his face. "Your cock is covered in blood, but I have an issue?"

I can tell he's trying his best to approach this situation with understanding and empathy. It's evident how upset he is. He and Micah have been searching high and low for him.

We've all been so worried. Frustrated.

Angry.

Damien just doesn't seem to understand.

He still seems lost.

Jensen meets my gaze, examining the small areas where I've been cut. "You alright, babe? You want me to kick his ass?"

"I'm okay," I softly answer. "No ass beating." Jensen nods in understanding, covering me with my robe and then wiping away my tears. "He just got home," I tell them. "I would've called you guys, but it took me by surprise."

"Don't worry. Asher called us."

"Are you sure you're okay, Quinn?" Micah questions, retrieving the knife from the floor.

"Yeah," I say. "Things just got a little heated, but we're alright. Really. I promise."

Damien visibly appears dazed as he looks over my naked body, his eyes glazed over.

"Damien..."

"It's Tuesday," he mumbles. "Isn't it?"

The air in the room becomes heavy. I swallow hard, trying to get a better grasp on what's taking place. Does he really... not remember?

Even with all the tension in the room, Jensen places a comforting hand on Damien's shoulder. "You should sit," he suggests.

"Just tell me."

"Sit, Damien—"

"No."

"It's Friday," Micah answers. "You blacked out."

My stomach sinks, a surge of disbelief coursing through me. But before I can say anything, Damien takes my hand. "Come on, princess. Let's unwind together."

BLOODBATH

"Damien," Jensen speaks up, following close behind us. "We need to talk."

"Quinn and I are going to take a shower."

Steam fills the air as we stand in the small confines of the shower. It's obvious to me that this façade of detachment after experiencing blackouts has become a coping skill for him. We've never spoken about this before and from the wall he has built up, I'm still not sure if he's truly ready.

A steady stream of water cascades down our bodies. The sound of the droplets hitting the tile creates a soothing atmosphere as we take turns lathering each other's skin with soap. A mixture of dirt and dried blood flows through the drain at our feet. I can't help the sadness that washes over me.

Just as quick as his eyes meet mine, I turn away from him, hiding my trembling lips and disturbed gaze. I don't want to make this any harder for him than it already is.

He steps closer until his chest is flush with my back. Lightly grazing his fingertips over the scarred initials on my hip, he holds me close, his lips beside my ear.

"I'm sorry," he vaguely whispers. "For scaring you."

"You... black out?"

"Yes."

I swallow. "We don't need to do this now."

"Yes, we do. I need to explain, especially since I put these marks on your pretty skin," he says emotionally, tracing the small wounds with his fingers.

"I wanted it," I defend, leaning back against his chest.

"That doesn't matter. I'm not me when I'm like that. I didn't even realize what had happened until I saw you bleeding. That won't ever happen again."

"It hasn't stopped you before."

"I'm different when I'm blacked out. I'm not myself."

"You used a knife on your dick, Damien. I'm aware."

He winces. "I don't remember any of it. That's why everyone has been looking out for me."

"Has it stopped bleeding?" I ask, but he stays silent. "Why does this happen to you?"

"I think it's from the trauma I faced as a kid. It started when I was pretty young, back when my mom was alive."

I gulp.

"It's heavy, Quinn. Real heavy. I don't want to unload my shit on you. You don't deserve that. You don't want to hear that shit."

"I want to know everything," I assure him.

He pulls me to him. "Everything?"

"Everything."

"The first time I watched my father kill a man, I was seven, and when I had my first kill, I was ten."

My heart shatters.

"He made me watch for a while, but that wasn't good enough for him. I wasn't a good enough son for him. Not until he gave me the knife. We hunted our victims at night and then secured them to a table in our basement. Mom knew what was happening. I know she felt guilty for not stopping it, but it wasn't her fault. He was a monster, and she was scared."

That does it. Tears spill from my eyes, and an echoing sob escapes me. Damien tightly wraps his arms around me and buries his face in the crook of my neck. I feel his pain so intensely.

He squeezes me tighter. "He hit me... a lot. Beat me pretty

much my whole childhood. He wouldn't beat my mom, but he did try once. I put a stop to it, though. Took the beating instead. It was my birthday. I was fifteen. Mom finally told me we were going to be leaving that night. I packed my bag and met Jensen and Micah at this stupid party to say goodbye." His voice cracks. "When I got back home... it was quiet. The piece of shit wasn't there. Mom and I were supposed to run, but I got there too late. She was on the floor... Her wrists were cut open... She was so pale. I thought she was dead. There was so much fucking blood. It was gushing out everywhere, and I tried so hard to stop it. Nothing worked. Not the kitchen rag. Not my shirt. Nothing. No amount of pressure would stop the bleeding."

"Oh, my God." I cry for him, visions of my own trauma from finding my father flashing through my mind. "I'm sorry—"

"I begged her to stay with me. I told her I was going to save her. I fucking promised I would save her. You should've seen the fear in her eyes. She was so scared, Quinn. I lifted her off the kitchen floor and carried her outside. I tried CPR. I tried to bring her back to me, but she lost too much blood. I watched as the light left her eyes. I had her tight. She died in my arms."

I sob helplessly, my heart breaking into pieces as I turn to face him.

"I fucking love you," he whispers sincerely, looking deep into my eyes. "I love you so fucking much." The second my lips part, he shakes his head erratically, frightened. "Don't say it back," he pleads, his warm lips kissing away my tears. "The only person who has *ever* loved me was the woman who birthed me, and I lost her."

"I'm so sorry," I whimper, raking my fingers through his hair, pulling him to me.

"Love..." he groans, pressing a gentle kiss on my jaw. "Love... terrifies me."

"Love scares everyone."

He draws back his head without warning. "What if I'm not good at it?" he asks, horror in his eyes. "I loved my mother... and she..."

He inhales a shaky breath.

Locking my arms around his waist, I hold him tight. "I know," I whisper. "It's okay, Damien. It's okay. I'm here."

"They say love is enough. But it isn't. It wasn't enough to save her. So please, don't say it back. Don't ever tell me you love me. Promise me right now."

"But Damien," I choke out, tracing the dimple in his cheek with my thumb.

"Her love for me... I killed her. Loving me got her killed."

"No," I argue, taking his face in my hands. He meets my eyes once more, but they've grown distant. "You did not kill her. Don't you dare put her death on yourself. That isn't fair. You were just a little boy."

He grips my wrist tightly, gritting his teeth. "She was trying to save me from becoming like him. Like my father. She was trying to save me. She loved me with everything in her. And loving me that much put her in danger."

"You're wrong. Love isn't what killed your mother. *Evil* is."

"Evil is in my blood, baby," he murmurs. "He's a sick fuck who gets off on torture. I get that from him."

"I don't care," I dismiss. "I don't care who your father is. I don't care that he's your family, or that evil is in your blood, because the only thing that matters is *this*." I firmly place my hand over his heart, feeling the steady rise and fall of his chest beneath my palm. "You told me I have your heart. Well, you have mine. You have *all of me*."

His eyes begin to glisten.

BLOODBATH

"Please let me say it. Let me tell you how I feel. You deserve love. Let me give it to you."

His mouth crashes against mine. He slips his arms beneath my legs and lifts me off the tile, bringing us under the steady stream of hot water.

"The things I've done," he lets out, his voice cracking.

My legs hug his hips, my arms snug around his neck. He holds me so tight, I can feel the pressure in my ribs.

"There's a place in hell for me, Quinn," he says against my lips, "but I'll die happy, knowing I had a taste of heaven with you."

"Damien," I beg.

"Okay," he whispers, the remaining pieces of his wall collapsing before my eyes.

"I *love* you," I confess, meaning it with every fiber of my being.

A tremor runs through him, his muscles flexing. He stares at me intensely, squeezing his arms around me, his nails digging into my skin, drawing blood on my back. He waits for me to vanish into thin air.

Waits for an inevitable black hole to sweep me away.

But it doesn't.

"I'm not going anywhere," I promise as his hold on me tightens. "I'm here to stay."

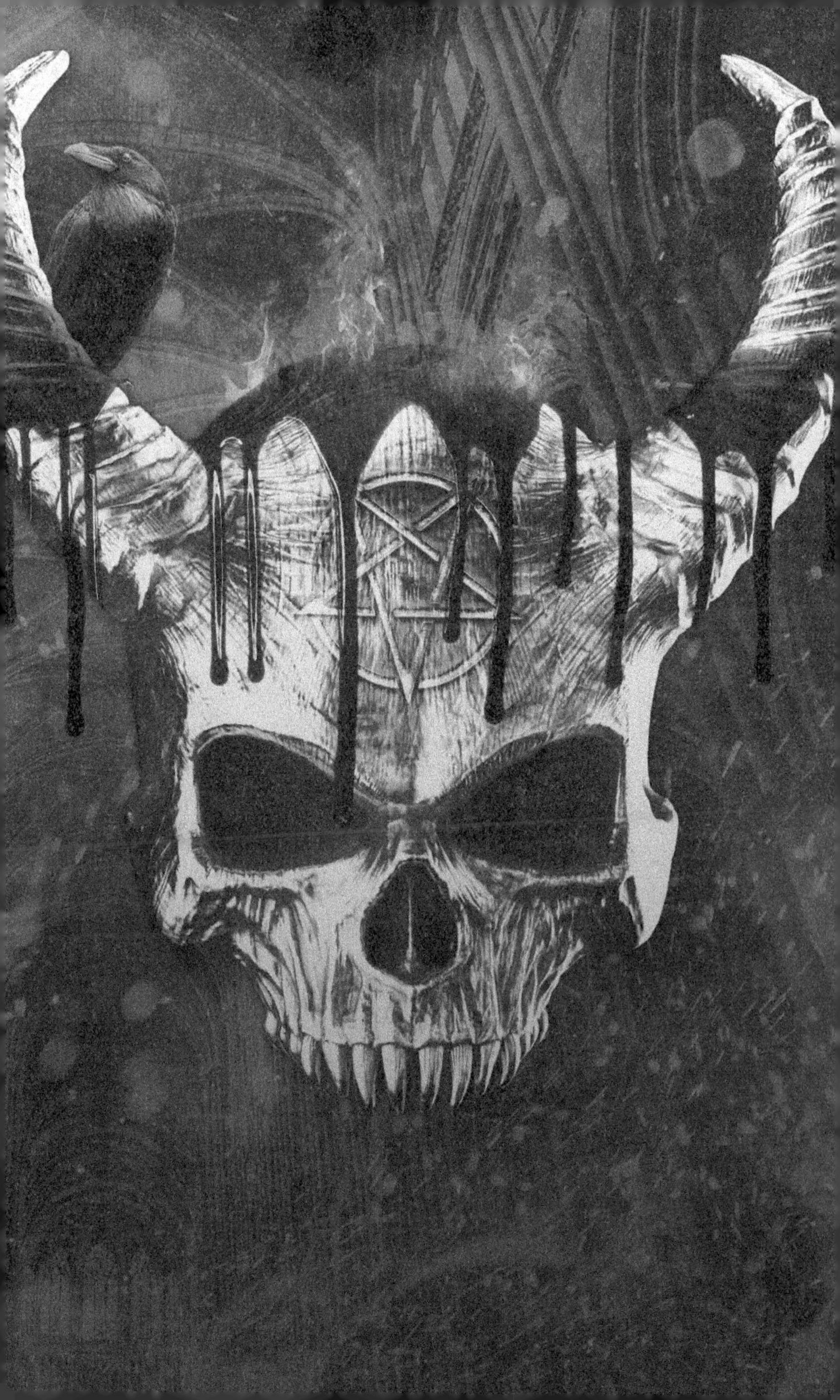

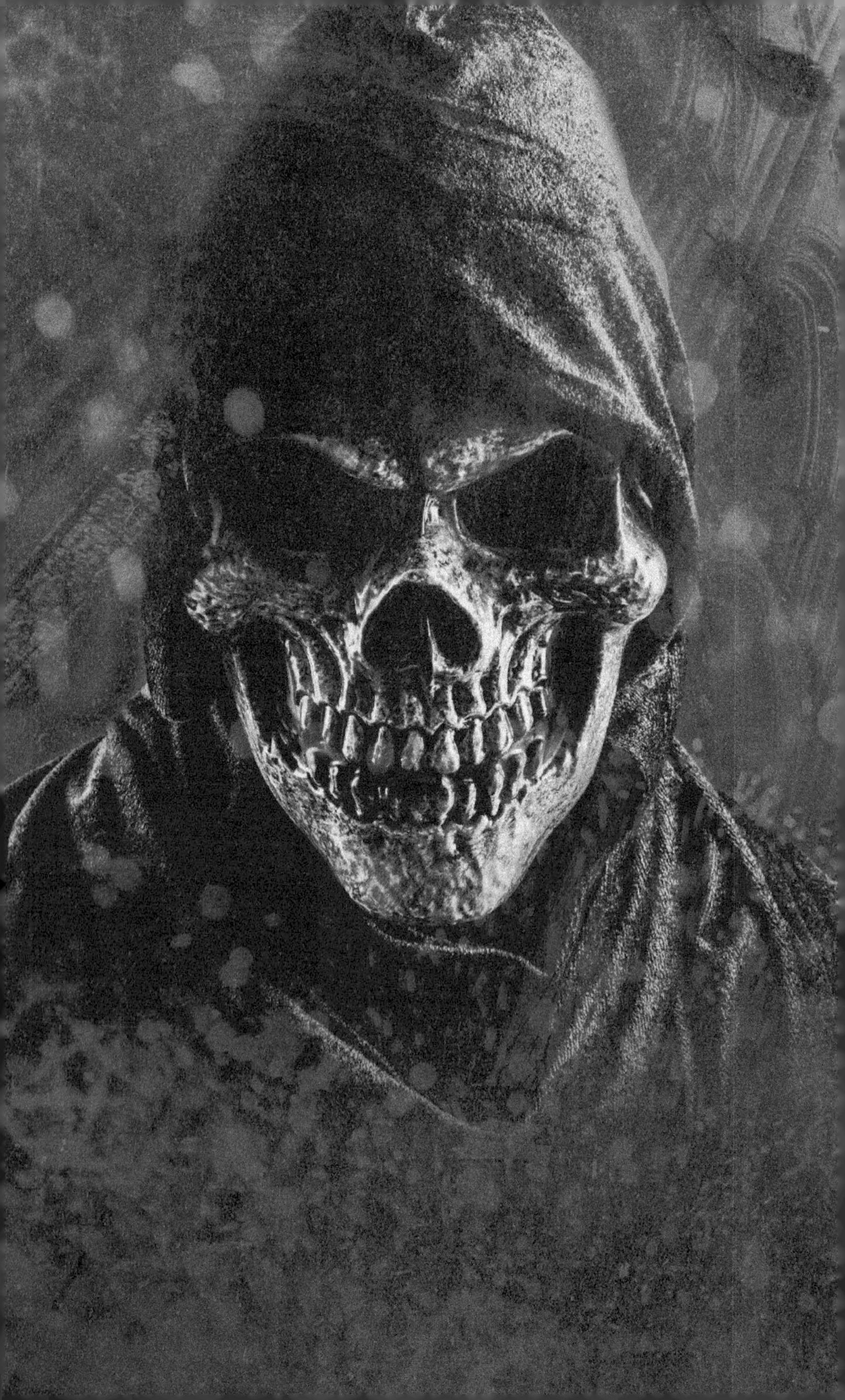

CHAPTER 10

DAMIEN

Darkness envelops us as Quinn and I settle into bed. With her face nuzzled in the crook of my neck, she drifts into the deepest of slumbers, snoring deeply. I know she hasn't slept in days and I'm the reason behind her exhaustion and worry.

I never gave my black outs much thought before. Not until now, this very moment, as I stare down at the woman I love. The knot in the pit of my stomach grows.

She's clinging to me, her nails digging into my shoulder blades and her breath softly caressing my chest with each exhale.

BLOODBATH

None of this is fair.

She doesn't deserve any of this.

Gently stroking her back, I nuzzle my nose in her hair, relishing the sweet aroma of lavender and vanilla.

"I'm sorry, baby," I whisper.

Pressing a soft kiss on her temple, I allow my lips to linger against her smooth skin, this sense of impending doom lurking in the room with me.

It's time. I know it's time for her to know the truth.

The whole story.

But I know before we say anything, we need to pay Genesis, the most important woman in her world, a visit. A visit she most definitely will not be ready for.

None of us are, though.

I'm on high alert when Jensen creaks open the door and slips into the room. Our eyes meet amid the darkness.

"Damien," he says softly.

"Not now. I don't want to leave her again."

"I know."

"I can't pull myself away."

"Try harder."

Looking down at Quinn, I nod reluctantly, hating myself fully and wondering how the hell I'm going to sneak away without disturbing her. I don't want to leave her here alone, but I have no choice.

I need to get caught up on everything that has happened since my black out.

She stirs slightly as I shift in the bed, sitting up slowly.

But she doesn't wake up. Instead, she snuggles deeper into the blankets and falls into a deeper sleep.

Exhaustion doesn't cover it. Quinn doesn't even flinch when I stand. Jensen patiently watches as I tuck her in tighter, draping the sheets and thick comforter over her bare shoulders.

I'm having the hardest goddamn time pulling myself away. I kiss her forehead once more. When her lips curl into a peaceful grin, I nearly melt.

Fuck.

Pull yourself together, Damien.

But hell, I can't, no matter how hard I try. Everything that has happened in my life has led up to this moment. Every choice, every mishap, good and bad. I wouldn't change a single thing, even the worst of it. Because at the end of the day, I was led to Quinn. She is my past, my present, and my future.

I've never loved anything more.

Quietly shutting the door behind me, I trail behind Jensen to the kitchen. Micah has been waiting, sitting patiently on the counter. He pours some bourbon into a glass and tosses it back.

"Enjoy your shower?" he asks smugly, his speech slurred.

I stare at him, but he has no interest in meeting my eyes. It's easy to tell he's filled with unprecedented rage. His face is beat red, the muscles in his jaw twitching. It's obvious he's trying to bite his tongue, when in reality he wants to lash out.

"Not particularly," I answer. "I spilled the beans about my great childhood. Abusive daddy and dead mom."

With dilated pupils, he finally lifts his gaze and glares at me from across the room.

"Easy, Micah," Jensen warns, his voice trailing off. "And put the fucking liquor away."

"It's fine," I tell him, taking long strides over to where Micah resides. "He's a big boy. If he wants to drink while he's on his meds, that's his choice."

Jensen drops his gaze to the ground, disappointed.

After grabbing a glass from the cabinet, and filling it with liquor, I sit so closely beside Micah that my knee brushes his. "You're pissed off."

"I am," he agrees.

"I get it."

"Ha. I'm sure you do," he scoffs.

"What's the damage? How many bodies?"

"Lost count. But don't worry. We cleaned up your mess, as usual."

"You wanna hit me or something?"

"Kind of."

"Go for it, then," I say, swirling the bourbon around the glass before bringing it to my lips. "I already got my lip busted open somehow. My eyebrow, too. Let's add a shiner to the mix. Is it cool if I get a little buzz first?"

"Get fucked."

"Fine," I sigh, standing with my waist between his legs, face to face. "Just do it."

"For fuck's sake," Jensen mutters behind me.

"I'm waiting."

"I'm not going to hit you."

"That's not what I was referring to. You told me to get fucked, so... do it. Fuck me."

"I'm not in the mood for your stupid jokes, Damien," Micah argues, gazing at me with disapproval. "I'm allowed to be pissed."

"You're right. You are," I reply.

He frowns. "I care about you, asshole."

"I know you do. I'm fucking sorry. I don't do this shit intentionally. I can't remember how it even happened. I grabbed a hold of the fucker when he came up behind me, and I couldn't stop hitting him," My eyes shut as I try to recollect everything that took place in that moment. "His blood was so warm on my hands. It felt like fucking heaven, if there even is such a place, but the rest is all a blur." Exhaling a sharp breath, I open my eyes. "Then I came back to… balls deep in Quinn."

"Her pussy brought you back, huh?" Jensen remarks. "Magical powers."

I shrug. "I'm telling you. I think she's a witch."

Before I can even wrap my head around it, Micah's arms are locked around me in a heartfelt embrace, his body warm and inviting.

I'm almost shocked by his gesture.

Cradling the back of his head with my hand, I breathe him in. "I care about you, too," I softly let out. Over his shoulder, I catch Jensen's eyes as he watches us empathetically. "I care for you deeply. Don't you know that?"

He nods, his body relaxing in my arms.

"You mean the fucking world to me."

"I hate you," Micah mutters, tightening his grasp on me, his fingers tracing the rippling muscles in my upper back.

There are so many times he has been my safe haven over the years. If I could, I'd shield him from the outside world. I'd do anything for him. My hands caress his back, too. I turn my head slightly, my lips brushing against his neck, this simple action conveying words I can't express.

But from the way his breathing quickens, I know he feels it.

It's impossible to dismiss the hot tension building between us. This moment of vulnerability lingers, several minutes passing us by. Words fall short here. He's seeking solace, unwilling to let go.

And so am I.

BLOODBATH

We park across the street from Quinn's family home the next morning. Micah and I approach the house cautiously as the sun rises above the horizon. We fear that we may be showing up a bit too early, but time is of the essence.

There's a hint of pine and smoke from nearby chimneys in the crisp air. I haven't spoken to her mother in a few years. I'd be lying if I said I wasn't nervous.

Micah glances at me briefly once we reach the front door. He seems really shaken up. The moment I take his hand in mine, our eyes meet. I wait for him until he's ready. Letting out a shaky breath after a moment, he nods. It takes me a few seconds, but finally, I ring the doorbell.

The door opens and she greets us sleepily.

"Hello, Genesis," I let out, noticing the fear that immediately flickers in her eyes.

"Damien," she wails, shaking her head with fear. "No—"

"Quinn is fine. She's safe."

The sigh of relief that leaves her sends a chill through my body from head to toe. With that, she opens the door and gestures for us to come in. The door shuts behind us hastily. We follow her to the kitchen and watch as she takes a seat at the table, placing her face in her hands.

"Give me a second," she says, her voice shaky. "I saw the two of you and immediately thought the worst. I thought you were here to tell me—" She lets out a choked sob. "—I thought something had happened to my girl. I need—a minute."

Micah and I exchange silent words with one another while Genesis gathers her thoughts. I lean against the doorway and lower my gaze to the hardwood floor beneath my boots, hating how we need to have this conversation with her. This is her worst nightmare coming true. We were all trying to avoid ever having to discuss this.

But the threat of the Hallowed Divine returning was always there.

The realization that this has now become our reality sends anger through me.

"They know," she murmurs. I nod. "How? How did they find out?"

"We aren't sure."

"I made a promise to my sister," she mutters, more to herself than to us. "I promised I would never let anything happen to Quinn..."

"Nothing is going to happen to her." She stares up at me with troubled eyes. "We would never let that happen."

"I promised I would keep her away from the society, and from what Quinn has told me, you've somehow made this personal."

"Genesis," I sigh.

"You're dating her?"

"Yes."

"You've gone against your vows."

"You're right," I admit, taking long strides across the room until I'm pulling out the chair and sitting beside her. "I went against my vow by getting personally involved." She nods in agreement. "But don't think for even a second that I regret it, because I don't." My tone is firm, her eyes widening in disbelief. "I don't regret any of it."

"How could you say that?" she snarls, teeth bared.

"How could I ever regret her?" I challenge. She stays quiet. "As far as I'm concerned, the Order is the last thing on my mind. She may have been just another order before, but she's so much more than that. All that matters to us is Quinn."

BLOODBATH

"Us," she echoes, locking eyes with Micah. "You agree with this?"

He nods. "I do."

"I want her to be happy. I care about her happiness," she rushes out, conflicted, tears building in her eyes. "If you make her happy, then so be it. I'm not going to take that away from her. God help me, I made a promise to her mother to keep her away from all of this, but she's fallen in love."

"Quinn needs to know," I urge. "She *deserves* to know the truth, and if Felicity were here, I have a feeling she would agree."

Her gaze drifts to the table. "Her whole life is going to change, Damien."

"I know."

"No, you do *not* know," she speaks over me, tears cascading down her cheeks. "She doesn't even know she's adopted."

I swallow hard.

"Oh, dear God. I've been meaning to tell her. I've been trying to figure out *how* to, but with telling her about her birth mom comes the rest of the story, and the rest of the story is going to break her heart." She looks into my eyes weakly, searching for the answer. "We'll never be able to go back after this."

"We won't," I agree, placing my hand on hers. "But by not telling her what's going on, we're only putting her more at risk. The Hallowed Divine knows about her. They've started their ritual. Severed head of a pig on her sorority's doorstep. Missing girls in town, all matching the same description."

Trembling, she covers her mouth with her hands.

"We would never make this decision without you. You're her mother, and I know you have the purest intentions. From day one you've only wanted what's best for her, and I want you to realize that you're not alone in this. We all want the same thing here."

"I know," she whispers, wiping away her tears.

"I love her," I confess. "I am in love with your daughter. I would give my life for her in a second."

"All three of us would," Micah chimes in. "I love her, too."

"All three?" She hesitates, an expression of confirmation overtaking her features. "I suspected she was leaving something out. Mother's instinct, I guess." A gentle grin crosses her face. "Come here, Micah," she instructs, gesturing to the chair closest to her. She pats his hand as soon as he takes his seat before her. "We've met briefly in the past, haven't we?"

"Yes, ma'am," he answers respectfully. "Shortly after we were given our orders."

"You also took an oath," she reminds him.

"I did. I vowed to do everything in my power to keep her safe. I never vowed to not love her."

"Touché," she mutters. "And where is Jensen?"

"With Quinn," I tell her.

"I want her to be safe, yes, but I also want her to be happy. You understand that, don't you?"

We both nod in unison.

She frowns, her voice turning somber. "She's happy. She's the happiest she's ever been, and here we are, about to take it all away."

Leaning forward, I look her straight in the eyes. "She's stronger than anyone. You raised her that way. She'll be okay. It's time, Genesis."

She turns to me, blotting at her tears with a crumpled tissue. "I'd like to be there when she learns the truth. As her mother, I feel I should be there."

"Of course," I concede, standing tall and placing a gentle hand on her shoulder. "She's going to need you there more

BLOODBATH

than anyone."

"Thank you."

"Would you rather tell her alone?"

She places her hand over mine. "I appreciate your asking. The three of you boys have kept her safe thus far. You've protected her. She loves you. We should all be there when she learns the truth."

"When?" I question.

"The full moon is only a week away." She wrings her hands nervously. "How about this weekend? Friday night?"

I nod, clenching my jaw once it finally sets in.

Three more days.

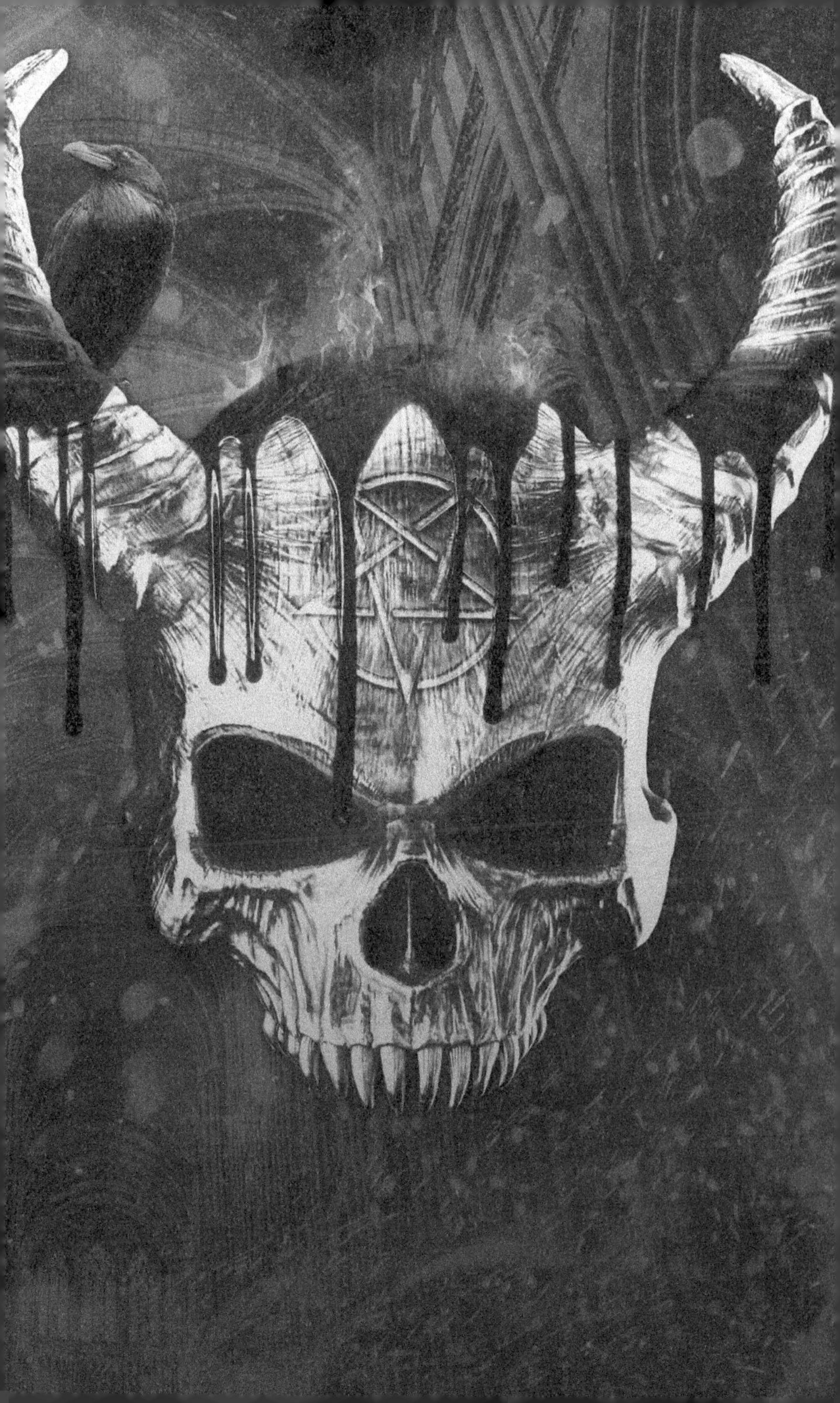

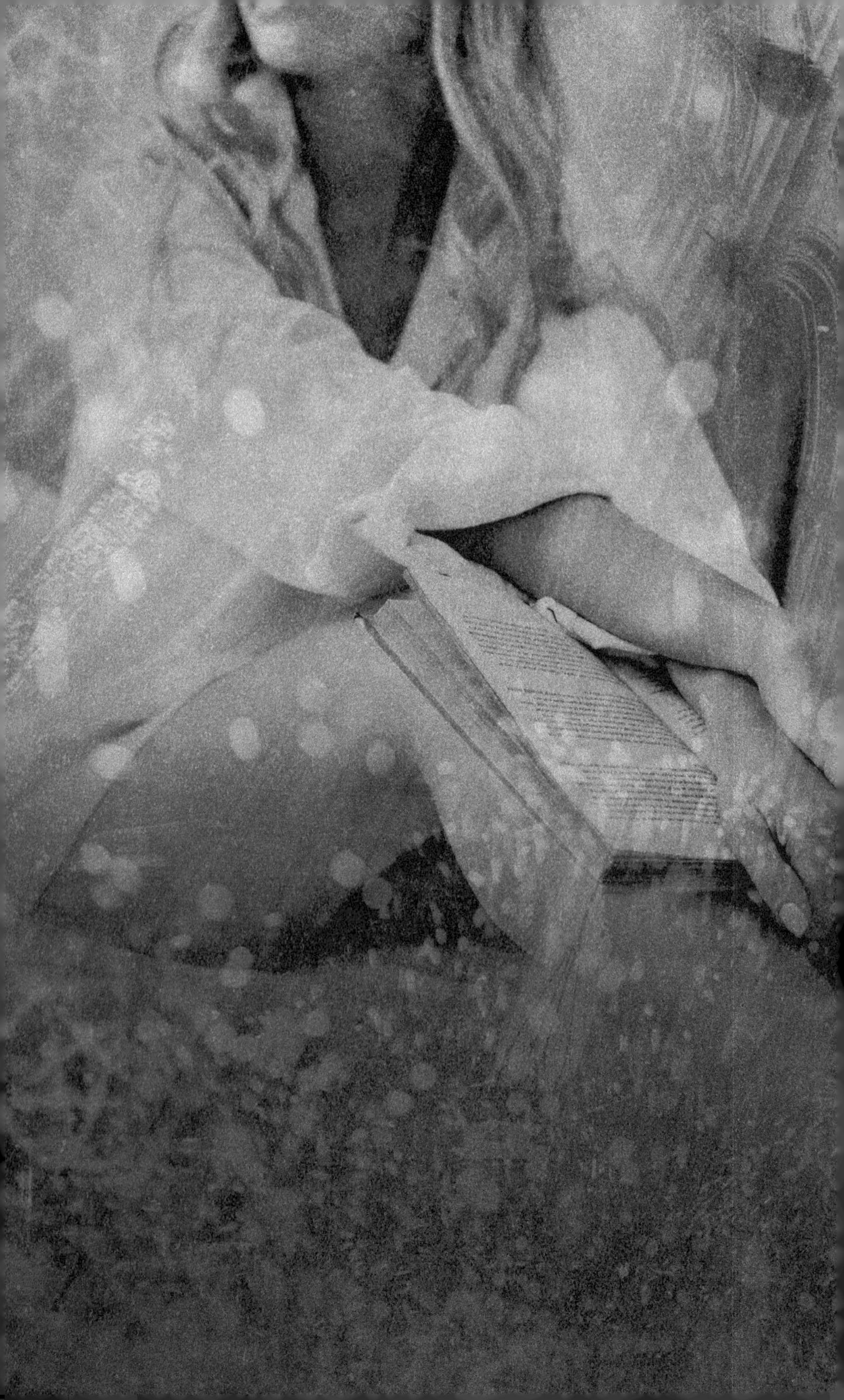

CHAPTER 11

QUINN

As I open my eyes to the light filtering through the curtains, I become aware of soft breathing from behind me. I know it's Jensen instantly from the crisp aroma of Irish Spring body wash. There's a peaceful stillness in the room as I wrap his arm around me tighter, nuzzling my face into his bicep. I turn my head, noticing his face softened by sleep.

Even though Jensen is the quietest of us all, he radiates such strength and safety. We all play different roles in this relationship. He has always been the backbone, the glue that holds us together, and I really admire him for that.

BLOODBATH

His tousled brown hair frames his face perfectly, his jawline strong and his full lips pursed. I let out a comforted sigh, overjoyed with his presence.

The last few days have been rough. I feel like him and Micah have been gone most of the time. I'm not only thankful Damien is now home, but Jensen, too.

I can tell how challenging this has been for him. I can't imagine how difficult it must be knowing your friend faces such awful demons and there's nothing you can do about it. The soothing sensations of the steady rise and fall of his chest against my back reminds me just how lucky we are to be alive.

Something terrible could have happened, but it didn't. Damien is back and all our relationships with one another are stronger than ever.

But why do I still feel as though we haven't escaped what is yet to come?

Caw. Caw.

The ravens call outside. It feels personal, like they're calling for *me*.

In his deep slumber, Jensen shifts closer to me, resting his chin on my shoulder. I press a soft kiss on his lips, realizing how long it's been since we woke up to one another without anyone else in the room.

I wonder if he knows how deeply I feel for him.

"I love you," I whisper.

Even though I know he's asleep, and hasn't heard my confession, a fluttering sensation fills my stomach. The warmth from the morning sun caresses my face as I grin to myself in blissful contentment.

Suddenly, he takes my hand, intertwining his fingers with mine.

"Please, say it again."

"I love you, Jensen," I confess.

He grows impressively hard, his erection pressing against the back of my thigh. I spread my legs eagerly, and he moves my panties to the side, the tip of his cock tracing along my slit, up and down, again and again. We both let out mutual sighs of need, the anticipation and desire building between us.

"I swear I loved you the first time I laid my eyes on you," he breathes, grazing his lips on the tender skin behind my ear. I welcome him fully. He slips inside of me so easily. Wetness pools on the sheets beneath us as he grinds into me, finding the perfect rhythm. A soft cry falls from my lips as he nips my collarbone, tracing his tongue along my skin. "It was two weeks before Christmas," he reveals, thrusting into me with deep, measured strokes. "I want to tell you how beautiful you looked, but you are so much more than a beautiful face and body." He quickens his thrusts, slipping his hand between my legs to work my clit. My mouth falls open abruptly. I gasp, trembling and moaning in his embrace, pushing back to meet his thrusts. "You're amazing, Quinn," he quietly lets out, applying more pressure, my arousal coating his fingers. "I loved you then, and I love you now."

He locks his fingers around my throat and drills into me deeper, the bed rocking with each thrust. Suddenly, my orgasm claims me, swallowing me whole.

"You like that?"

"Yes," I whimper.

"Such a good girl for me," he moans, my inner walls contracting around him intensely. "You're coming so hard, baby. Your pussy is gripping me so tight."

The pleasure is so intense I can't even speak.

"So fucking wet. Rock your hips, baby, just like that," he encourages. "More…"

"Oh my God," I helplessly cry out, seeing stars behind my

eyelids.

"Good girl."

With his face resting in the crook of my neck, he spills himself inside me, burying himself deep. Holding me close, he kisses my shoulder.

"You really said it first," he murmurs.

"I beat you to it." I trace the muscles in his forearm with my fingertips, giggling softly.

Soon enough, I drift back asleep in his arms.

I can sense the darkness in the room even before I open my eyes. Night has fallen. Surely, I couldn't have slept the entire day away.

Right?

Quiet chatter sounds from the hallway. Rolling onto my side, I set my gaze on the faint light and shadows from beneath the door. It's a challenge for me to make out what they're saying, so I slip out of bed and tiptoe across the room. Eavesdropping, I press my ear to the doorframe.

"Just let her sleep for now," Micah suggests. "She's exhausted."

"I know," Jensen sighs. "Poor thing hasn't slept in days."

"Because of me," Damien says, shamefully. "Because of the hell I put her through—"

"It wasn't just her. Yeah, you scared the fuck out of Quinn, but you also scared the fuck out of Micah." Jensen hesitates briefly, letting out an exaggerated sigh. "And you scared the fuck out of me, too, man. The whole damn society was on edge."

Society?

"Three fucking days," he adds. "The worst possible timing."

"I know," Damien snaps. "You act like I can control it."

"Can I ever express how I feel, or is it always about you?"

For a moment, there's an uncomfortable silence between them.

Jensen continues. "I understand it's out of your control. But when you lose your marbles and disappear like that, leaving a trail of bodies behind for us to clean up, it puts a lot on Micah and I."

"Yeah," Micah agrees. "Not only having to follow you around but us also having to sit in your place at the table."

"And this time… shit was bad."

"Bloody."

My stomach cramps, bile rising up my throat.

"She's been asking questions over the last few days," Jensen reveals. "Questions we haven't been able to answer. Like who was the figure standing outside her window? Who has been following her? Who left the note on her pillow? What do we really do for work? If we tell her we're just trying to *keep her safe* one more time, I'm sure she's going to end up biting our dicks off."

"Well, here I am," Damien declares. "I'm back, okay? Now we can answer them."

"When?" Jensen asks.

"We agreed on Friday."

Not a chance in hell am I waiting another second.

Suddenly I'm standing before the three of them, staring them dead in the eyes. They look like they're seeing a ghost. They weren't expecting me to put them on the spot like this, yet they were stupid enough to have this conversation in the hallway right outside the bedroom.

"Quinn," Damien says, his voice calm. Soothing.

BLOODBATH

He knows it's over. He's been caught.

"Why wait until Friday?" I question, my arms folded tightly over my chest. "Answer them now."

Jensen and Micah glance at one another.

"I'm done with the secrets. I'm so fucking done. If you guys don't come clean about what's really been going on, *right now*, then I'm gone. I'll make sure you never find me again."

This is the first time I've ever seen real fear in their eyes. True terror.

"You think I won't walk away?" I test, exchanging glances with each of them. I stare grimly into Micah's eyes. "I might have been naïve when we first met, and yes, I ignored every red flag," I rush out, watching as Jensen sinks beneath my scrutiny, "but I can't look away anymore. I refuse to. I deserve better than this shit. You all love me? Then stop keeping things from me. If we're going to be together, then we need to be honest with each other." Staring up at Damien once more, my face hardens. "So, tell me."

Without hesitation, he replies. "It's better if we show you."

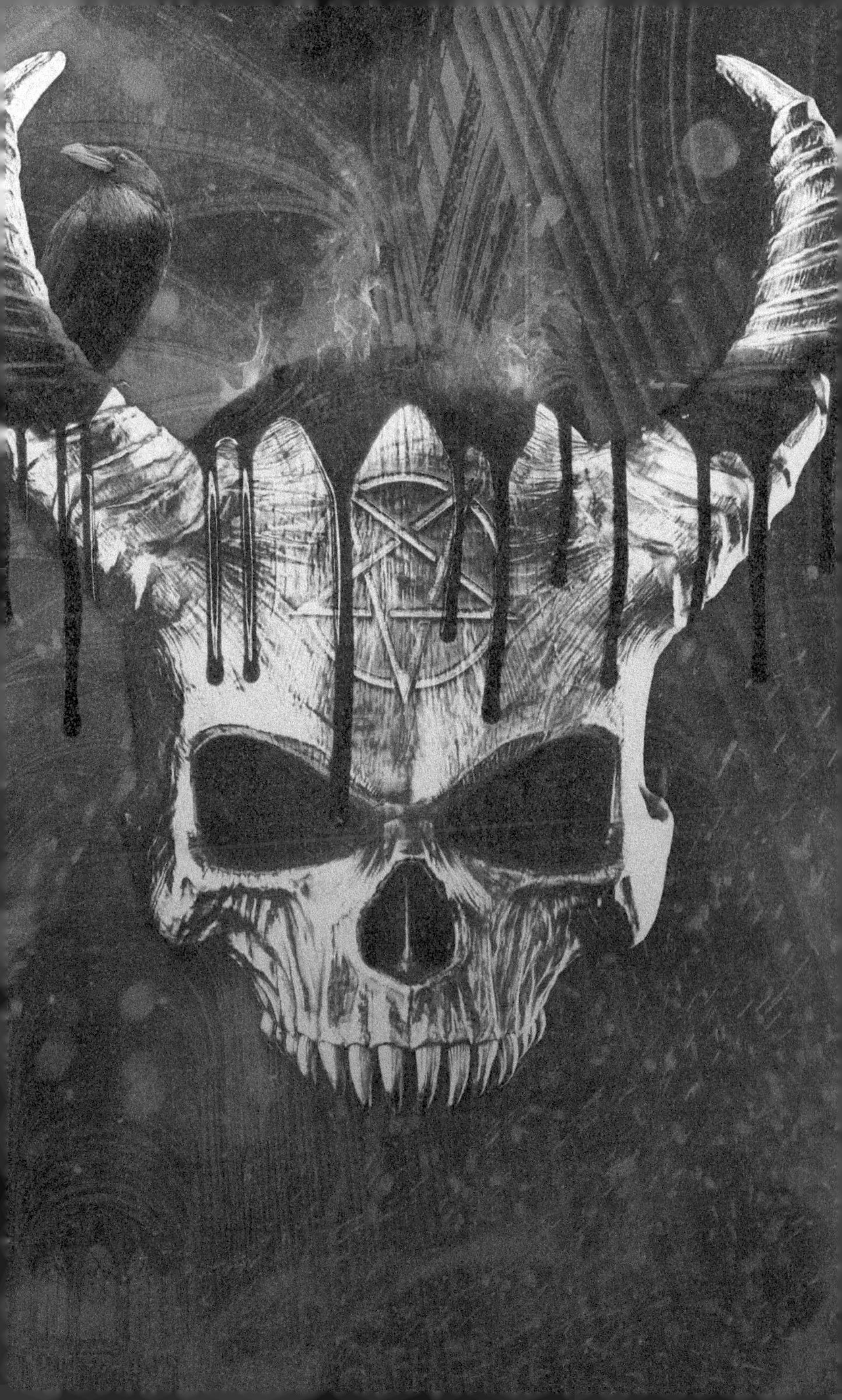

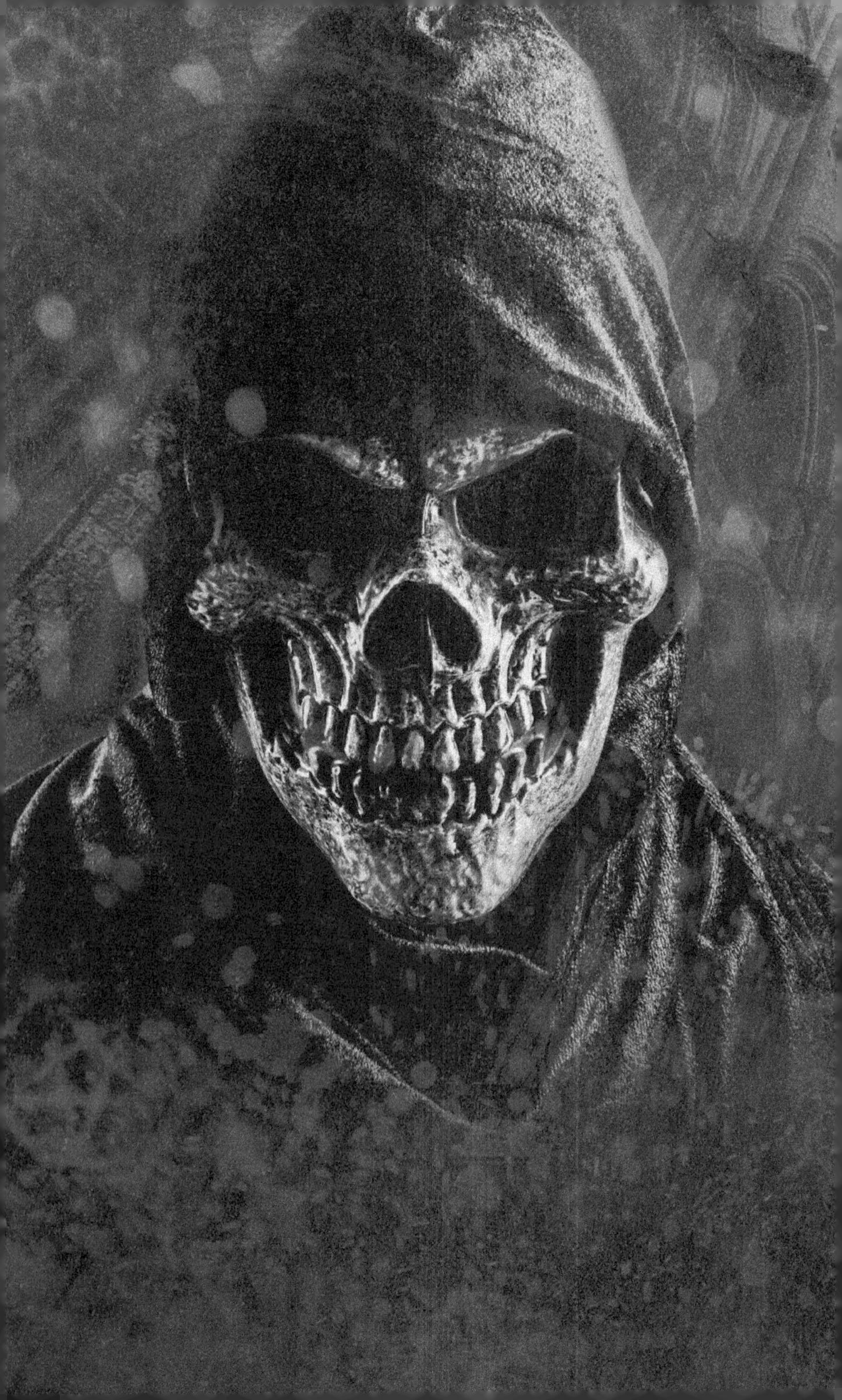

CHAPTER 12

DAMIEN

Tension builds between the four of us as we approach the club. Sinsations is just about a block away and yet I haven't even considered what I'm going to say to her. Quinn is smart, and man is she livid. The second my hand meets the top of her thigh, she pulls away, proving my observation correct.

I don't say a word. She has the right to be upset. For all the months she has known us, she has suspected that we were hiding something from her.

It's not like we were hiding a small truth.

This isn't like lying about shitty credit scores, past

relationships, or not seeing their text or call.

This is Quinn's life at stake. We can blame it on the Order until our faces turn blue...

You were an order at first, princess, but you've become so much more.

We took an oath of secrecy, baby.

Babe, if we told you sooner, it could have done more harm than good.

But no. Trust or not, that's all bullshit. None of that will ever be good enough in Quinn's eyes, and that destroys me.

I rest my chin on my tightly clenched fist, staring out the windshield into the dark, gloomy night. I'm not a good guy. I never have been. But, hell, I really tried to be better for her.

She shifts in her seat, hugging herself tightly, as if she's seeking the feeling of security.

A hushed "Quinn," escapes my lips.

"Don't," she warns.

The dull organ that resides in my chest *aches* for her. The urge to pull her onto my lap despite her probable rejection is almost overpowering. I park the Jeep at the curb beside the club and look her way, searching for the right words.

"Everything is going to be okay," I promise. She avoids my gaze. "Look at me, baby." My little Quinn shakes her head, reaching for the door. "Please."

"No—"

That's when I redirect her attention toward me by cradling her face with my hands, giving her no other option. She explores my eyes with anger and frustration in her own.

"What do you want, Damien?"

Tracing my thumb over her pink, pouty lips, I say the first thing that comes to mind.

"I want to make sure you hear me fully when I say this," I begin, emphasizing every word. "Who I am in there is *not* who I am when I'm with you."

She blinks innocently at me.

"There's a difference between guys who say they'd kill for you, and guys like me who actually do it."

Her eyes glisten.

"To the world, I am a menace to society, but what I am to you is the only thing that matters to me." My tattooed fingers curl tighter around her jaw. "I would do *anything* for you, whether it's gutting someone who has wronged you in the past, or burning this whole town to the ground just so they never have the chance."

"They're here, Damien," Micah announces. "I just got the text."

"What? It's after four in the morning," Quinn mutters, alarmed. "Who's here?"

I hop out of the Jeep and jog around the front. As soon as I open her door, I can sense her uneasiness. She seems distant, and rightfully so. Except it's the blatant horror behind her gaze that eats at me.

She leaps straight into my arms and clings to me. "Hold me. Please. Just for a second."

"Okay," I say softly, caressing the small of her back.

"I just want you to hold me before we go in there—" She cuts herself off.

"Because this might be the last time," I finish for her. "Depending on what we've been hiding, you might leave us. Is that right, princess?" She tries to draw back, except my grip on her tightens. "You could walk away, baby, but just know, we will *always* be one step behind, killing anyone who touches you."

I reluctantly release her.

Jensen places his hand on the small of Quinn's back, shooting me a nasty glare.

BLOODBATH

Sinsations is almost pitch black when we step inside. I switch on a light and slow my pace as Micah pulls me behind.

"Killian is tied up," he quietly explains.

I arch a brow. "Do you mean that literally or metaphorically?"

When Quinn and Jensen turn the corner, Micah takes hold of my bicep and yanks me to a stop. He looks me dead in the pupils, as if he has something important to tell me, but his lips remain in a firm straight line.

Immediately, I'm on edge. "What?"

"They just found three bodies outside town hall."

"Great," I snap, trying to remain collected. "What does that mean, Micah? I need more context. Are they mine? Did I fuck up?"

"No. They aren't yours. Killian and a few of our guys are on watch. The cops have the place surrounded. The whole thing is all over the news."

"Three bodies," I echo dryly. "Let me guess. They're all the missing women?"

He nods somberly.

The next step in the Hallowed Divine's ritual.

Two young women disappear, then before anyone even has time to report the third, they're all found dead.

Resisting the urge to put my fist through the large glass window beside us, I pinch the bridge of my nose between my fingers.

"Damien," he murmurs, slowly trailing his hand from my bicep to my shoulder. It's evident there's something he hasn't told me from his reluctance to continue.

I frown. "Just give it to me, Micah."

"Their wrists have been slit. They're all carved up, man. They've been fucking mutilated. The photos got leaked."

My body becomes numb. I try to fight away the gruesome image of my mother lying in a puddle of blood.

I sway to the side, losing my balance.

Micah swiftly grabs hold of me. "You're okay," he soothes, keeping me grounded.

The vision hits me.

The gaping wounds in her wrists.

"You're good," he reassures me. "Say it."

Her blood soaking through the towel. My shirt.

I'm good, I mouth silently, my fingertips digging into the nape of his neck.

"I got you," he whispers.

The light draining from her eyes.

Her body going limp.

My soul turning pitch black.

After all these years of not speaking to my father, he's still taunting me.

Squeezing my eyes shut, I stumble again. Micah guides me backward until my back is pressed to the concrete wall. He positions himself so his body is against mine—chest to chest, face to face—with his knee between my legs. He grabs my jaw and makes me look at him.

"Don't let the memory take you," he warns, eyes narrowed. "Stay with me. Okay?"

With a nod, I stare into his expressive eyes. Those rich, warm hues of amber.

A range of feelings sweep over me as I look at him. I find myself wondering if he feels it, too. The magnetic pull that seems to draw us closer together lately. The force that has me trailing my hand up his forearm in a desperate attempt to feel him better.

His heated gaze drifts to my mouth, and he lightly traces my lips with the pad of his thumb. All I need is his warm, gentle touch to bring me back from the darkest pits of hell.

I don't fight the gradual shift of emotions that wash over

me, the growing feelings I have for Micah. But it's a new dynamic of our relationship I'm not yet inclined to act on.

I shake away the thought until there's only one thing on my mind.

I am going to find my father, and I'm going to kill him, as well as anyone who stands in my way.

"You good?"

"Yeah."

"Okay." Micah clears his throat and steps back. "There's more. They left a message in blood. We think it was meant for you."

He hands me his phone, and my chest tightens at the image.

She follows

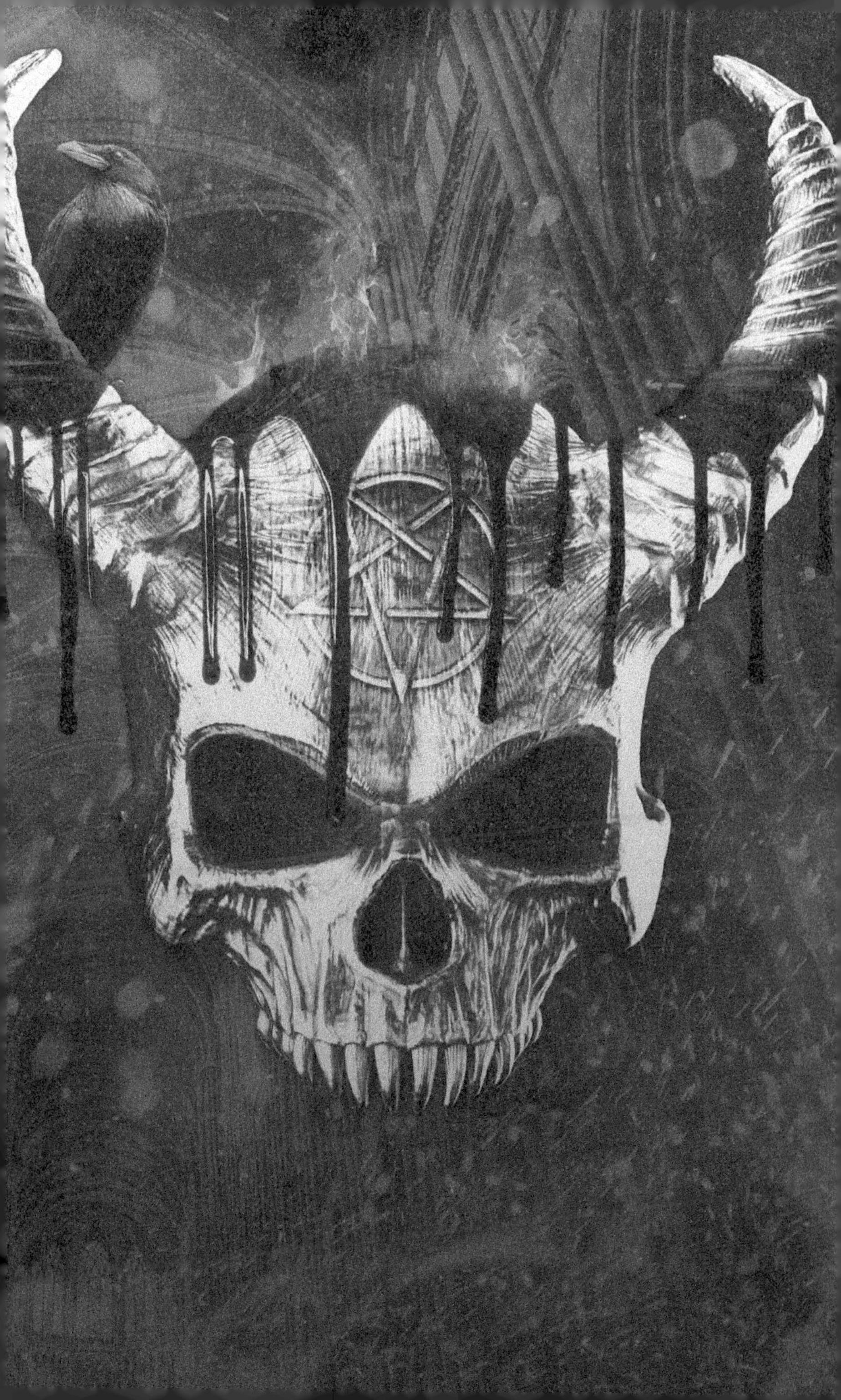

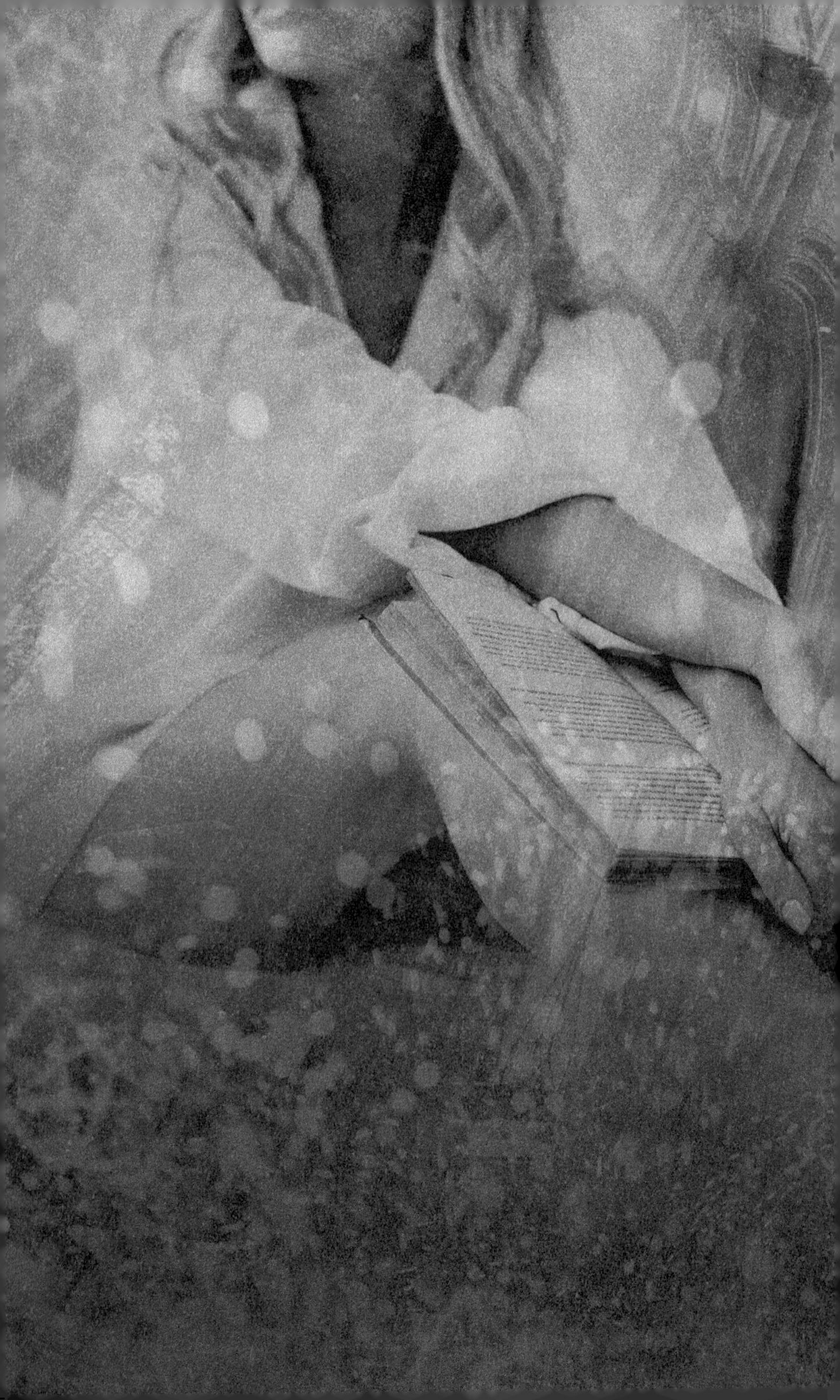

CHAPTER 13

QUINN

As I step into the room on the lower level of the club, all the hair on my body stands up. It feels otherworldly in here, like I'm suddenly the leading role in some kind of movie or theatrical performance. The air is heavy in the dimly lit area, a shroud of secrecy enveloping me like a weighted blanket.

This place appears to be an exclusive sanctuary of sorts. Countless shadows are cast along the walls, and as we make our way further into the large room, I stop dead in my tracks.

We aren't alone. There are figures in what feels like every direction, their identities hidden by precisely crafted masks.

BLOODBATH

Skulls, to be exact.

They're so still I begin to question if they're made of stone, but the hushed whispers and flowing robes as they shift sends me into fight or flight mode.

I step backward, flinching from fear as my back collides with something firm. Masculine hands grip my hips, and I know it's Jensen right away simply by the scene of his cologne.

"You're good," he says, his lips beside my ear.

Swiftly turning on my heel, I lean into his chest, accepting his embrace.

An uncanny silence hangs in the air. As intimidated as I am, it's hard to not feel intrigued at the sight before me. Damien takes long deliberate strides further into the room, and the masked figures appear to be engaged with him fully, their attention fixated his every movement.

There's this sense of importance and urgency that permeates the room. Impending danger, possibly? All the gut feelings I have had recently of being watched by someone... or something... strikes me right on cue.

The severed pig head on my sorority's doorstep.

The dark figure lurking in the shadows on campus late at night.

The note on my pillow.

The mask with devil horns.

1, 2... we're coming for you...

My blood runs cold.

"What is this?" I question.

"This is the part in the story where your life changes."

"Who are you really?"

My heart begins pounding with each step he takes toward me. "Who are we?"

I nod and whisper, "Yes."

He places a finger beneath my chin and tilts my head back.

"The Order of the Unseen."

A chant breaks out, *"Unknown. Unspoken. Unseen.:"*

"A secret society founded by my uncle, with the sole purpose of keeping people safe." Damien hesitates briefly, his eyes narrowed, tracing my lips with the pad of his thumb. "But more than anything... keeping *you* safe."

"Me?" He nods slowly. "From what?"

"Evil," he answers. "We took an oath in blood. We've been protecting you from a cult. They go by the Hallowed Divine. My father is one of them."

My whole world crumbles.

I was right.

All the research I've done...

"I was right," I say aloud, slipping into a state of shock. "Oh my God."

"The chain of disappearances and unsolved murders over the years," Micah begins. "The Hallowed Divine is behind all of them. What Damien is telling you is true."

My heart races. "I... I did research myself... It sounded so crazy, but I figured maybe it could be what's going on... and now that you're finally telling me this, confirming it, it just sounds even more insane..."

They watch me closely as the remaining pieces of the puzzle fall together.

"The dark figure in the mask, they're one of them," Jensen reveals. "Along with the three men that were outside your window."

Suddenly, there's a sinking sensation in my stomach. "So, let me get this straight. You're telling me there has been a *cult* after me, one that has been kidnapping and killing people for *years*, and you never thought to even *mention* it until now?" I demand, my voice growing louder and angrier with each word. "Are you serious?"

BLOODBATH

Words can't even express how horrified I am.

"Please tell me you're joking. Tell me this is all just another lie."

"No more lies," Damien tells me. "The secrets are over. Just like you said. You want the truth, so here it is."

Fighting through a sense of mental fog, I turn my back to them, scanning the room full of dark figures in masks. You would think I'd be shaking with fear, but instead... I find myself experiencing a kind of tranquility amongst the shadows I never knew existed.

I don't feel threatened. Not one bit.

If anything, I feel as if I've wandered into a safe space.

A part of me feels like I'm no stranger here, almost like I've been here before. Maybe in a past life or a dream.

This only seems to make matters worse. I can't wrap my head around any of this. This is all so much information in such a short period of time... It sounds crazy. Like this is some kind of made-up story... A nightmare, even. Finding a reply is too much pressure, especially considering all the glowing eyes are focused solely on me, tracking my every move.

"I'm supposed to be your girl. You're supposed to tell me everything. Not keep secrets from me when I have a target on my back!"

When Damien steps toward me, I move away.

"Don't come near me!" I warn. "Fuck. Fuck, fuck. I need a minute. Maybe even a lifetime."

"Okay," he says.

I find myself trying to make a run for the door, only to be cornered by the large, daunting figures that step out from the shadows. I squeal, leaping back.

"They're not going to hurt you," Micah says. "They would never hurt you. We're family here."

"Family?" I demand, glaring in his direction. "You've kept

me hidden from them. These people are supposed to be your family, yet you hid me from them! Are you embarrassed of me?"

"It's not like that, baby," Micah tells me. "This entire society's purpose the last few years has been to watch you. Protect you from harm's way—"

"That does not sound reassuring, Micah!" I shout. "It just sounds like you all are a bunch of stalkers! Why didn't you just bring me here sooner? You didn't trust me to be around them until now? Is that it?"

"Trust has nothing to do with this," Jensen objects.

"Trust has everything to do with this," I shoot back. "I knew the three of you had a bad rep and that you were into some bad shit. That you're fucking dangerous. I wasn't naïve about that." Suddenly, I'm fighting back tears, keeping myself together to the best of my ability, even though my whole world is falling apart. "But then I told you I love you, and this whole time... I was *a job* to you?"

Fear ignites in their eyes, my voice loud, erupting off the walls.

"All this time... you were ordered to keep tabs on me. *Keep me safe*," I mock, cursing the tears that spill from my eyes. I fix my attention on Damien. "How did you choose me? Eenie meeny miney mo?"

His face hardens instantaneously.

"What? Is that a soft spot?" I demand, standing my ground. "Why me, Damien? Why am I so important to the society? Surely you can tell me that. Honesty, right?"

A strangled breath travels up his chest.

"Damien," Jensen growls, his voice tight.

"Not yet," Micah presses. "We promised her—"

"Promised who?" I stress, my voice dropping. "Her?"

"No, fuck," Damien hisses, closing the space between us

so quickly I have no time to react. He curls his fingers around my biceps with a vise grip and pulls me into him forcefully. "It's not like that, Quinn." I try to push him away, but he's too strong. "It's not what you're thinking, baby. Get out of your head."

"Then who the fuck is *her*?"

"Your mother," he says in a whisper.

"Damn it, Damien," Jensen shouts, furiously. "We made a deal!"

"My mother?" Blinking at him, my pulse quickens, the blood swishing in my ears. Damien's face softens. "What does my mom have to do with this? You're talking to my mother behind my back?"

"We promised her that we'd wait."

"Wait for what?"

"I can't tell you, yet, baby. I'm so sorry."

A blind rage fills me. "Let go of me," I order.

"Never," he callously bites out, his chest firm against mine. "Maybe in another universe, but not this one."

"Damien," I snarl.

"I will *never* let you go, Quinn. Not even when I'm dead."

"Don't you love me?"

He winces. "Do you have any idea what you're asking of me?" he urges, his grip on me tightening. "Let you go? That goes against every aspect of who I am—"

"Do you *love me*?"

"Yes. Yes, Quinn. I love you."

"Then show me. Let me go, Ghost."

Damien becomes completely immobile. His mouth opens in a silent gasp, his breathing slow. Shallow. Even with the soft lighting, I watch his pupils dilate, his face draining of all color. My simple request has him battling the demons within him trying to break loose.

Distinctively, his grip on me loosens, his body language displaying pure panic and uncertainty.

With terror in his eyes, Damien releases me.

"Don't follow me," I warn, pointing an angry finger between the three of them. Scanning the room of masked figures, I search for the nearest exit. "None of you follow me. Or so help me God, I will…" I inhale a shaky breath, desperate for the ache in my chest to dissipate.

"Quinn," Micah begs.

"If you guys love me like you say you do… then give me space."

Jensen steps forward, blocking my only way to the door, a line of tall figures towering behind him. "I do love you, but please, they're after you," he argues, his eyes darkening. "The missing girls… they turned up dead. They're dead, Quinn. There's no way in fucking hell I'm letting you become—"

Suddenly, he stops himself. A heavy silence takes over the sanctuary. Jensen looks into my eyes painfully as I approach him, and within seconds, he steps aside. Neither of us have to say another word. We're in a mutual understanding that I am not backing down.

"So be it," I state. "Let them come for me."

Jensen recoils, staring straight over my shoulder, his distraught eyes fixed on Damien.

I wait for Damien to say something.

Anything.

Silence hangs in the air.

The soft sound of footsteps echoes from somewhere behind me. I squeeze my eyes shut, feeling a light breath on the back of my neck. I know that presence immediately.

My Damien.

He's so close, I can almost feel him, reaching out for me, his hand lingering in the air above my shoulder. There's a

BLOODBATH

painful longing between us, a connection so profound that time as we know it freezes. The world stops spinning on its axis. There's a gravitational pull so intense, it threatens to throw me right back into his arms.

His palm brushes my skin, ever so lightly, and a static shock erupts through my body. A sudden reminder from the universe that sometimes the things you want most in life can hurt you.

"Let her go," Damien calls out.

The solid wall of dark shadows divides into two, allowing just enough space for me to get by. I stumble down the narrow path, growing more impatient by the second, and fumble with the access key on the door.

Can't get it open. Can't get it open.

Why won't it open?

Two large veiny hands come into my view.

Their fingers move swiftly as they enter the passcode. Taking a risk, I gaze up at the person towering over me. Even with the mask obscuring their face, I'm immediately met with a pair of dark, cryptic eyes. We share a stare so intense it almost sends me to my knees.

At this moment I find myself unable to move, as if my feet have been permanently cemented to the ground.

I never expected to feel so connected to one of the members, especially considering I've never met any of them before.

Except... *I have.*

My stomach sinks. I know these eyes. How could I ever forget looking into them the night they seemed to be my only source of comfort?

"*Asher*," I whisper.

Pure disbelief and betrayal creeps up on me. The society has been around me all along. I just didn't know it. A sensation of unease devours me. There's a tinge of worry behind his gaze, a preemptive warning. I can feel him begging me to stay.

To not make any rash decisions that I'll later regret.

Without thinking it through, I brush past him and hurry through the doorway, feeling disconnected from the world and everything around me.

From the men I've grown to love.

The men who have been intentionally keeping me in the dark for as long as I've known them. I resist the urge to puke. Letting out a small sob, I break into a full sprint down the dark isolated corridor of the basement without looking back.

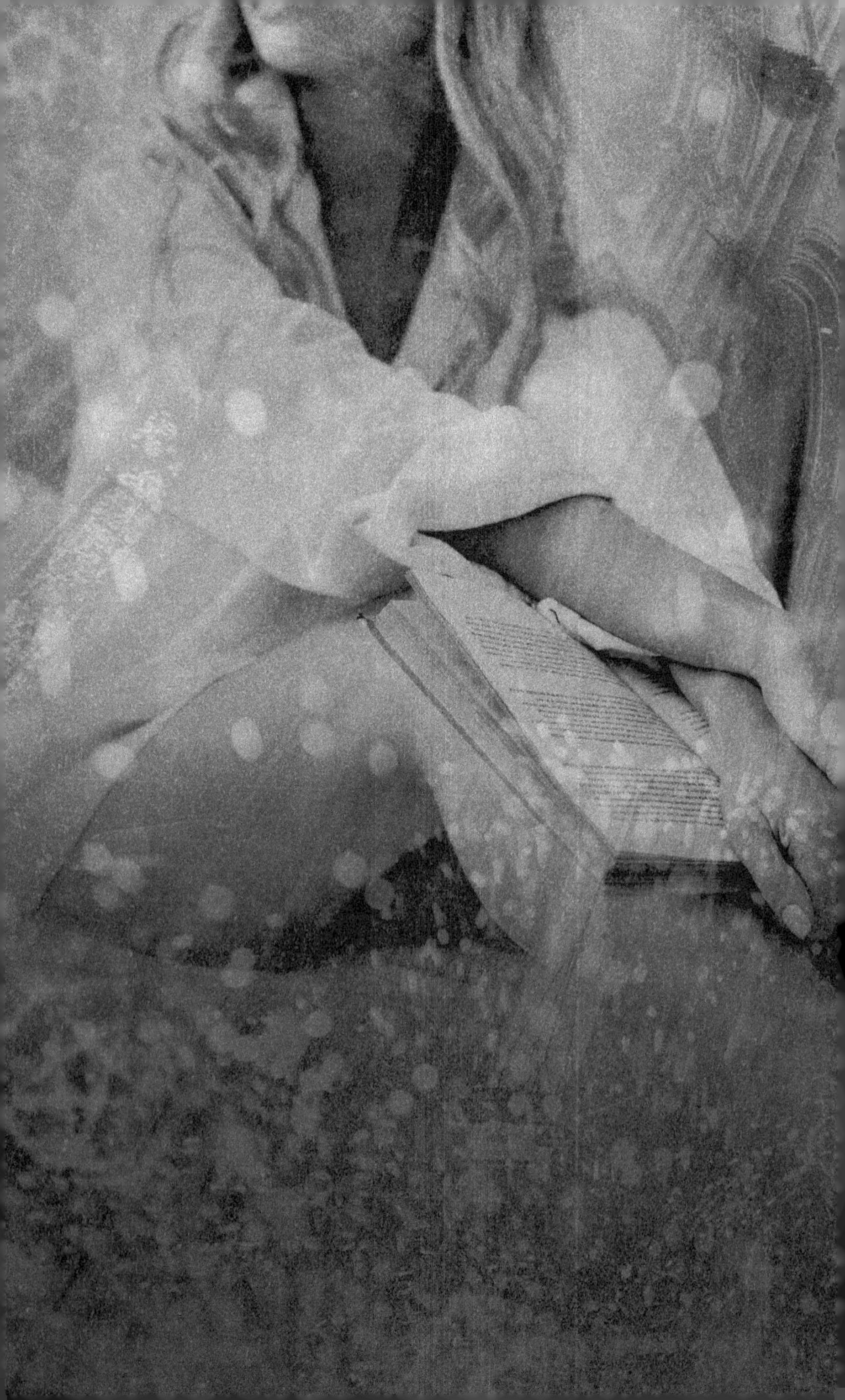

CHAPTER 14

QUINN

Nothing was a coincidence.

Meeting them at the Halloween party.

Damien finding me in the library the next morning.

My mother's bizarre reaction to hearing Damien's name on Thanksgiving.

The pig head on my doorway.

The feeling of constantly being watched.

The missing girls.

I run down the dark, quiet sidewalks of Boston while raking my brain, trying to make sense of everything. My

BLOODBATH

mind races a hundred miles a minute. My boyfriends being involved in a secret society doesn't surprise me. Perhaps that's something I'd be able to look past.

But hearing that this whole time they've kept something so important from me, it makes me question what else they've been hiding.

Am I doing the right thing by running away?

Have I ever truly confronted any of the problems in my life?

My mother has done her very best by keeping me sheltered from the dangers that lurk around each corner, and to hear that she has been talking to the man I love behind my back... I'm not sure if I'll ever be able to understand.

I should have asked right then and there, but I couldn't stand to be anywhere near them for another second. Anger doesn't even begin to express how I'm feeling.

Since I know there's a strong chance they're not going to listen to me and give me the space I have asked for, I want to get as much distance as I can *while* I can.

Until they find me.

Eventually I find myself hiding in a quaint little café downtown, sitting at the table in an uncomfortable silence.

"Here you go, enjoy."

"Oh, I'm sorry," I murmur, attempting to hand the plate back to the barista once they set it down on the table. "I didn't order this."

"Someone else did."

"Who?"

They shrug.

A gust of icy wind sweeps through the café, except the door hasn't opened, the heat is blasting, and the windows are nowhere close to where I'm sitting. The hair on the back of my neck stands up, goosebumps rising on my skin.

"Thank you," I reply softly, my gaze focused on their back as they walk away.

Confusion sets in. Besides the two employees and I, the café appears to be empty.

Not having thought of them for a while, and after finding out I was right about there being a cult all along, I retrieve the notes from my purse. I place them on the table, studying them defeatedly.

Knock, knock.

"Who's there?" I challenge myself aloud.

The abrupt sound of a chair scraping against the floor makes me flinch in my seat. Damien sits across from me, flashbacks from the morning after Halloween replaying in my mind, when he followed me to the library and told me I was his.

"Haven't you learned anything? Never say 'who's there?' Don't you watch scary movies?" He taps his thumb on the side of his styrofoam cup, a smirk on his face.

"What? I told you I needed space—"

Wait.

My body stiffens.

His voice seems… different. Raspier. My gaze zooms in on his hand. My pulse quickens and my body stiffens. It takes my brain a moment to get through the disorientation I'm experiencing. The outline of bones on his fingers is what's catching me off guard. They're new tattoos, but they're slightly faded.

And I've never seen that ring before.

He must notice my attention trained on his hand because he flexes it briefly, stretching out his fingers. I reach forward and grab his wrist, flipping his large, veiny hand over to examine his palm.

The scar is gone.

BLOODBATH

"But it's your right hand," I mutter, the blood pumping vigorously through my veins. "What the... hell..."

He yanks his hand away. "You shouldn't be grabbing strangers like that."

I gawk at him in disbelief, noticing the small scars on his face, and the crow tattoo on his neck.

All I can do is blink. I've become frozen, glued to my chair. *Strangers.* I study the situation that is unfolding before me, taking in every detail of the man sitting just mere feet away.

He looks deep into my troubled, puffy eyes.

I gulp. "Damien?"

"Wrong, but lucky for you, I'll give you another shot."

"You're not..." He shakes his head. "But then..."

"I'm not him."

What the fuck? What the fuck?

What the fuck?

The small difference in facial features should have been enough to give it away. Other than that, his body shape, and the absence of the dimple on his cheek, he looks *identical* to Damien.

But this is in fact *not* the man I love sitting before me.

He arches a brow, taking a sip of his drink casually, as if my whole world being flipped upside down right before his very eyes doesn't faze him one bit.

"What the fuck," I finally say aloud, not knowing whether to run and scream or remain seated in the safety of this coffee shop. "What the fuck!"

He lets out a sharp, noticeable groan, as if he's annoyed, catching the leg of my chair beneath the table as soon as I try to escape.

"You... you look just like him..."

"Well, we *are* blood."

I put two and two together, staring at him incredulously.

"Damien has a brother?"

"I'd say I'm surprised he's never spoken of me, but that would be a lie."

"A twin—"

"Still wrapping your head around this?" He sighs impatiently, leaning back in his chair and folding his arms. "I'll give you a minute."

"This is a cruel joke."

He looks around with a grimace. "Nobody's laughing."

"I have to be dreaming."

"Not dreaming."

"I am," I rush out. "I'm dreaming."

"You're not, though," he confirms loudly, reaching across the table to pinch my arm. I squeal, glaring at him while rubbing away the discomfort. "See? Not a dream. Now can we pick up the pace? You don't have much time."

They look so alike, it's uncanny. I continue to look him over, slipping further and further into disbelief.

"Time is of the essence, Quinn," he remarks, his voice dropping. "I don't have all day. I've got places to be and people to torture."

I lean back, creating more space between us.

When I don't respond, he reaches forward and snaps his fingers in my face. "Listen here. I'm going to lay it all out on the table for you and you can do what you want with it. Alright?"

Shaking away my dismantled thoughts, I try my hardest to stay in the moment. "Can you start with your name?"

He has the same crooked grin as Damien, but it doesn't meet his eyes.

"Omen."

"Omen," I echo.

"Good girl. Sound it out."

I scowl at him, the rage I had been feeling earlier consuming me once more. "Excuse me for not coming to terms with this in a timely manner that suits you," I snap. "It's already been a fucked up last few days, and then you show up out of nowhere—"

"Well, I hate to break it to you, but it's about to get more fucked up."

"It gets worse?"

"It does." From the look in his eyes, I know he's not lying. "The Hallowed Divine. You know of them?"

My eyes widen.

He mimics me. "I'll take that as a yes. I should start off by letting you know I'm a member."

"You're in a cult?" I demand. "*The* cult that's after me?"

"Yeah, but that's beside the point."

"What do you mean it's beside the point?"

"I couldn't give a fuck about your involvement in the ritual. I've been done with that for a while now. I've gone... What do they call it? Rogue?"

"I'm supposed to believe you?" I challenge, eyeing him. "I don't even know you."

Omen leans forward, his eyes locked with mine. "Believe me or don't believe me. For you, it's life or death. The only thing I'm getting out of this is maybe some peace of mind." His eyes turn into small slits and his brows become furrowed. For a fraction of a second, he appears to be in the deepest of thoughts before dragging himself out of it. "Maybe," he reiterates.

"Everyone in my life has been keeping stuff from me. Even my mom."

"Well, she's dead, so she doesn't really have a choice."

My heart sinks. "My mom is dead?"

"She has been for a while. You look just like her, by the

way. It's... a bit creepy, actually."

Time freezes. The room spins. I feel like I'm going to be sick.

Omen frowns, confused. "We're talking about your birth mom, aren't we?"

Birth mom?

"W-what?" I practically whisper. "Birth mom?"

He says nothing.

"What are you talking about? I'm not adopted."

He pokes his bottom lip out. "But... you are."

"I'm not. You have the wrong person."

"Jesus," he snarls, running a hand through his dark, wavy hair that's mostly slicked back. "I know this is hard but try to keep up. Her name was Felicity. She was originally a member of the Hallowed Divine, but ended up having a... change of heart... over time. Cult life wasn't for her. Shit got too dark. She had a weak stomach, couldn't handle the things she saw and had to do, blah blah blah—"

"What the hell are you talking about?"

"Can I finish?" His eyes grow cold, sucking the life out of me. "Long story short, her relationship with our leader resulted in, well, *you*. She kept her pregnancy hidden and sought out refuge from the cute little secret society your boy toys are a part of. Nine months and some change later, a baby girl was born."

"With the leader of the cult?" I inhale sharply. "That can't be true. This isn't real. This isn't happening."

He rests his chin on his tightly clenched fist, his eyes darkening.

"Because that would mean..."

Omen remains silent, watching me put it together.

"My... birth dad... is the leader of the Hallowed Divine."

"Bingo."

BLOODBATH

"What you're telling me is that my whole life has been a lie," I choke out, the saliva thickening in my mouth. "My entire fucking life has been a lie. All of it."

"Yeah, yeah. Condolences, whatever."

Tears cascade down my cheeks as I think about my mom, the wonderful woman who raised me. The woman who gave me the best life she could.

I think of my father as well, the man who gave me everything I asked for. The man who spoiled me rotten. The man who ultimately chose to leave.

And then I think about the suspicious circumstances of his death that was eventually ruled a suicide.

My gaze meets Omen's once more.

"When I was younger… my dad took his life."

"Did he? Or was it taken from him?"

As soon as the words leave his mouth, I break into a quiet sob. This is all too much to deal with at once.

"There, there. Don't let your pastry go to waste," he mumbles, pushing the plate toward me. "I know it's your favorite."

How does he even know that? I don't respond.

I just seem to cry harder.

For the life I once knew that has now come to an end.

"Listen. I don't have all the answers, but I do know what both our fathers have planned." He reaches across the table and snatches my phone. "You'll need someone from the inside, so I'm adding my number. You'll have some convincing to do with Damien."

"Why are you doing this?" I ask, searching his eyes. "Why are you telling me all of this?"

Omen cocks his head to the side, slowly sliding my phone back to me. There's a vacancy behind his gaze I can't quite explain.

MOLLY DOYLE

"You remind me of someone," he breathes, his voice low.

"Your mother?" I assume, drying my tears with the sleeve of my sweater.

He grimaces. "No, Quinn. Stop that. I don't have a mother. I never did."

I frown. "You never met your mother?"

"I was raised in the church since I was an infant. Barely saw the sun. It's the reason I'm so pale."

"This isn't the time for jokes," I complain.

"I'm not joking."

"Did you... know my mom? The one who... birthed me?"

"She raised me. Made me promise to look out for you if the time ever came."

I stare at him in awe, desperate to learn more. "Are you the one who has been following me recently?"

He nods.

"You're the one who stood outside my window in the red mask," I accuse, becoming flustered at the memory of it. I flashed him. He saw one of the most intimate parts of me. "You were stalking me on campus and followed me back to the sorority."

"Stalking?" he scoffs, seeming annoyed.

"Well that's what it was. You're the one who has been watching me and leaving me notes."

"Guilty."

I frown, thinking back to them.

Knock, knock.

You're supposed to say who's there.

"You and your shitty joke," I mutter dryly. "So all I had to do this whole time was say 'who's there?' That was your cue to just... pop in?"

"Easy, right?"

"I assumed it was Damien playing tricks on me during his

black out. I figured he just didn't remember."

"I'm not fond of my brother. I'll admit that, but I'm even less fond of my father. I can't stand that prick. I'm sure that's the one thing Damien and I have in common."

"What did Damien ever do to you?"

He forces a cold smirk. "What *didn't* he do?"

"I can't help if you don't tell me."

"I don't want your help, nor do I need it."

I look away, fidgeting nervously with my hands. "He's been lying to me. They all have."

"Well, yeah," he says with a shrug. "Probably to keep you alive, but fuck them, right?"

"I can't believe you're sticking up for them."

"Call it whatever you want. I'm just pointing out truths. Even the hard ones."

"Is this all just a façade to gain my trust?"

He snorts under his breath. "The last thing I care about is your trust."

"Then why the hell are you here?"

"Because we both want the same thing, Quinn."

"And what's that?"

He leans forward with ominous eyes and bared teeth. "Retribution. I know deep down, you want it, too. Maybe not now... but you will, Quinn. With time, you will."

"You say that with such certainty. But again, you don't know me."

"If you're anything like Felicity, you'll want nothing more than to burn the Hallowed Divine to the ground. It still needs to fully sink in. Give it time. A day or two, and you'll come running."

"You've got it all planned out."

"I do."

Ding. Ding.

The door of the café opens.

Omen quickly glances over my shoulder.

"Quinn," three voices call out for me.

Leaping out of my chair, I turn around to find Damien, Micah, and Jensen rushing toward us. When their gaze sets on Omen, time seems to stop. I take everything in with the little time I have.

Jensen and Micah look horrified, like they're having some type of out of body experience. It's immediately clear that they also had no idea he existed.

But Damien... His eyes are pitch black. "Omen," he blurts out, horrified.

Omen grimaces. "Well, this is awkward."

"Wait—" Jensen snaps, his eyes nearly bulging out of his head.

"How the—" Micah gasps, his eyes darting back and forth between the two of them. "What is this?"

"What the fuck..."

"What the hell is happening?"

"Why the fuck are you here?" Damien demands, leaping in front of me. "What do you want with her?"

Omen scowls. "I don't want anything."

"Bullshit," he coldly snaps. "If you touched her... even laid a finger on her... I will—"

"You'll what?"

"Damien," I rush out, my hand latched onto his shoulder.

"What the fuck are you doing here, Omen?"

"Having a heart to heart with Quinn, clearly. Can't you tell? We're in tears over here. Bonding and shit."

"I warned you to stay the fuck away. If this is a set up, I will tear you to shreds. Hell, I'll do it regardless."

"Yeah?" Omen pushes out his chair without warning. "I'd like to see you try."

BLOODBATH

"Stop!"

Ignoring me, Damien steps forward, enraged.

Omen strides toward us, his stance tense. They're only seconds away from ripping each other's heads off. I place myself between the two of them and grab hold of Damien's face.

"No! I need him alive. He didn't touch me. He's done nothing wrong."

"You're crying."

"Not because of him. I'm crying because I finally know the truth. He told me everything. Something the three of you should have done a long fucking time ago."

Damien meets my gaze in return. He looks so defeated, his face flushed, and an intense heat radiating from his body. He's sweating profusely, as if he's just been searching the whole city for me. The muscles in his jaw are rippling with anger, a vein protruding in his forehead.

With a sharp breath, Damien backs away, pulling me along with him. "I don't trust him," he tells me.

Omen lets out a dry laugh. "The feeling is mutual."

"You cannot trust him, Quinn."

"Who the fuck are you?" Micah directs at Omen. "Damien? Fucking talk to us. You have a brother?"

"A fucking *twin*," Jensen adds in, not taking his eyes off him.

"To my dismay." Damien focuses on me once more, gripping my hips and holding me close. "Baby—I-I don't know what to say. Can we talk about this… after?"

"What the fuck?" Micah snaps from beside us, fuming.

"No, Damien, we can't," Jensen retorts. "This needs our attention *now*."

My head begins to spin. We're all dealing with different realities at the same time. My life has been turned upside down. Jensen and Micah's, too, all for different reasons.

"I'm sorry." Damien drops to his knees without warning, wrapping his arms around my waist and holding me tight. "I was wrong. Tell me what to do. Please, baby. What do you need right now? I'll give you anything—"

"You were protecting me. My mom, too. I didn't understand that until now. Why couldn't you have told me sooner? Why keep things from me for this long? Why lie?"

He stares up at me with glossy eyes. "Because I'm a fucking idiot. That's why."

"Everything I just learned... I can't believe this... You have a twin... Not to mention he's involved with the cult that's after me. This is insane."

"He's what?" Micah exclaims.

Omens gaze burns through me. Even though I refuse to meet his eyes—those cold, dead eyes—I can feel him watching my every movement.

"Fuck this shit. Fuck your family reunion, and fuck you," Micah barks at Damien, torn apart. He turns away and heads for the door. Jensen shoots Damien a disappointed glare before following in his trail.

They exit the café together. My heart shatters once I get a true grasp on how badly this has affected them.

Omen watches the scene unfold with a devious smirk, entertained by the chaos.

"Well," he mutters, "now this is *really* awkward."

"Can the three of us go somewhere to talk?" I ask.

Omen furrows his brow. "I mean I'd rather not..." he mutters, his voice trailing off.

"Then get the fuck out of here," Damien snaps, glaring at his brother.

Omen scowls. "Why are you so stubborn? We can help each other. I'm offering my services free of charge. Don't you want to take them down?"

"You're one of them. You belong to those fuckers."

Omen's voice turns hard. "I don't belong to anyone."

"Just stop it," I demand. "Both of you." I fix my gaze on Damien, feeling an emotional turmoil I haven't felt in a while. "I feel lost right now. I'm so angry. So heartbroken. I'm adopted? The woman who birthed me is... *dead*? My mom has known all of this, this whole time... and my dad? Did he really kill himself? Was my dad murdered? Who killed him? Why?"

"I'm so sorry," he whispers painfully, rushing back to his feet and taking me into his arms. "I'm here. Okay?" I accept his warm embrace, the wetness from my tears soaking into his shirt. "I should have told you sooner. I fucked up. Bad."

"Yeah. You did."

"I know," he breathes, cradling the back of my head. "I made a promise to your mom. I gave her my word."

Sneaking a glance over his shoulder, I search the café, finding that the two of us are suddenly alone. From the corner of my eye, I spot something from outside the nearest window. Omen stands outside, peering in through the glass, just like he did that night with the devil mask.

We hold an intense stare, and even though my heart is shattered, and my world has been forever changed, I can't help but feel released.

If I had gotten this news from the men I love, I'm not sure I would have been able to look at them without being reminded of all the lies I've been told throughout my life.

Omen took that role knowingly.

"Hey, princess?" Damien questions softly. "It's time I show you something. Can I take you somewhere?"

I look into his eyes. "Okay."

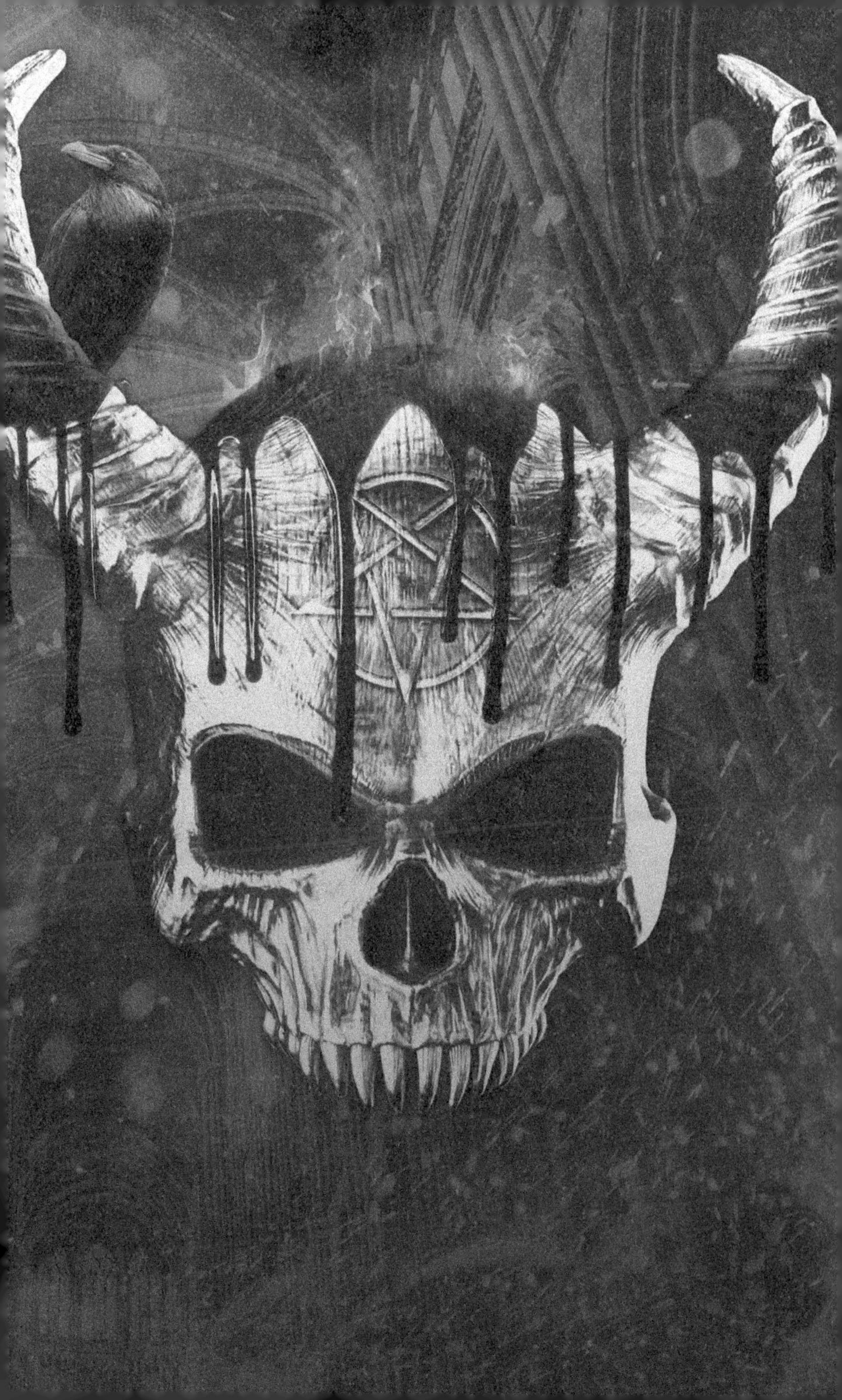

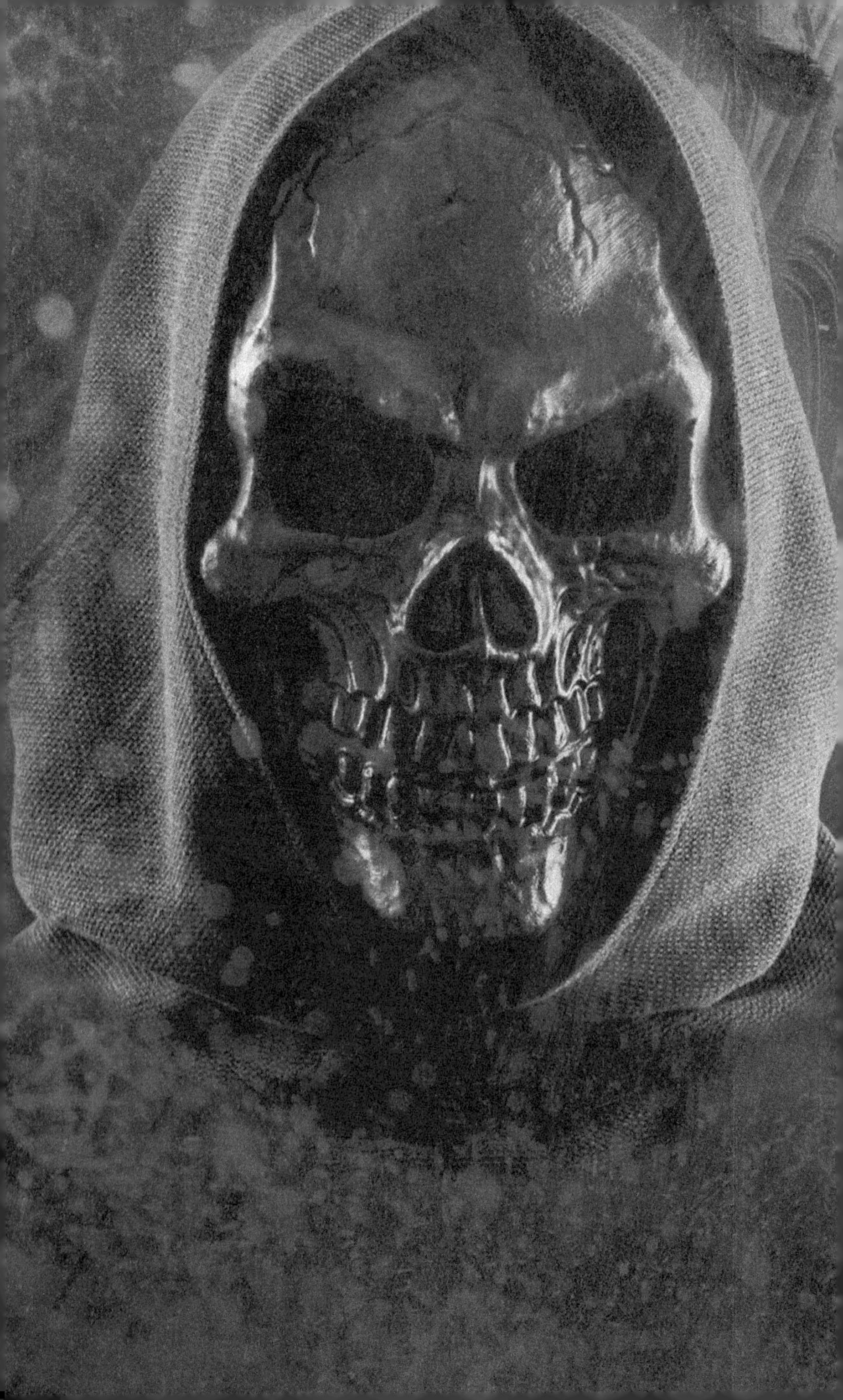

CHAPTER 15

JENSEN

The crisp air bites at my skin. Anger doesn't even describe what I'm feeling right now. The intensity of emotions I'm experiencing is difficult for me to comprehend. The violation of trust, the utter disbelief, and betrayal? I thought I knew him better.

Damien has always been guarded, and there's parts of him I'm sure nobody would ever be able to understand.

Can I sympathize with him?

Sure.

But it's hard to accept someone keeping something so important from you.

BLOODBATH

In a jog to keep up with Micah, I curse my legs for not being longer. It's hard to see him like this. The three of us have built such a strong foundation of friendship over the years, but they've always had a bond, allowing them to connect on a deeper level.

I'm kind of surprised he didn't know.

If Damien was to tell anyone, it would be Micah.

"I want to get fucked up," he mutters. "I need a drink."

"You can't drink on your meds," I remind him.

"That would only matter if I was on them."

Quickening my strides, I search his eyes, although he keeps his gaze forward. "What do you mean? You haven't been taking your meds?"

"Nope."

I blink at him, shocked. "What the fuck do you mean?"

"Jensen," he snaps, irritated. "Can we not do this right now?"

"Micah."

"This is a problem for another day."

"You should've talked to me," I press. "We're not kids anymore. Why didn't you say anything?"

For a brief moment, our eyes meet, and... fuck. *If looks could kill.*

"You know I hate how they make me feel," he argues.

"I know that. We've been over this."

"A lot of shit's been going on. I've had a lot on my mind."

"You know you can always talk to us—"

"Yeah? Damien never talked to us. Looks like we're all real good at keeping secrets, huh?"

"No. Don't fucking do that," I exhale sharply, catching his wrist with my hand. He tries to pull away, but I just grip him tighter before pinning him up against the brick wall. He glares at me, his eyes small slits. "Don't act like an asshole. I didn't do anything to you. If you want to be pissed at anyone, then be pissed at Damien."

"I am," he shoots back. "I'm fucking livid. We've known him since we were kids and he never even thought to mention having a brother? Not to mention he's a literal twin, so identical it makes my skin crawl... but his own flesh and blood being a member of the Hallowed Divine? All this time? Not only his dad... but a brother, too? Those sick fucks are after our girl! We've been protecting her for years. *Years*. We all took oaths. He should have fucking told us!"

His eyes frantically search mine, as if he's waiting for an answer.

"I know. I'm upset, too. I'm still processing all of this."

"I mean, fuck," he snarls, pushing me away. "I thought he told us everything. I don't even know who he is right now."

"He's still the same person. He must have a good reason."

"Doubt it."

"You're angry right now. You just need some time to think."

"And Quinn," he rushes out, his complexion draining of all color. "She's going through absolute hell right now, and all I'm thinking about is myself. I'm so fucking selfish." Out of nowhere, he smacks himself in the face. It happens so quickly I don't have time to stop him. Until he does it again and again.

I leap forward, taking grip of his wrists with such strength I can imagine I'm leaving bruises. He tries to fight me off but ultimately fails.

"Stop that! Stop hurting yourself. You don't deserve that. If you want to hit someone, then hit me."

"That's the last thing I want."

"You've come a long way, Micah. We all have. It's because we're a great fucking team. We've kept each other in check since we were kids," I remind him. "We look out for each other. Nothing will ever stand in our way. Not unless we allow it to."

He rests his back against the brick wall, slowly sliding down until he's sitting on the icy pavement.

"Look where we are right now," I point out.

The memory comes rushing back to me, the time Micah tossed a brick straight through a store window, sending glass everywhere. We took off running after the alarm got tripped and eventually ended up here, in this very alleyway, out of breath with adrenaline pumping through our bodies like nitrous.

Micah looks around for a moment and then nods in realization. "Shit. It's been a while, huh?"

"That was the first time I saw you have a manic episode."

"Full blown," he adds dryly.

My chest twinges. "I was worried about you. I cared about you then, and I care about you now."

"I know you do," he whispers.

"Your lips are turning blue. Let's get you out of the cold, yeah?"

After a long pause, he sighs. "Okay."

He accepts my hand and I help him to his feet. Once I pull out the lighter and pack of cigarettes from my jacket pocket, he erupts into laughter.

"Rainy day," I tell him. "You never know."

He grabs the back of my neck and pulls me in, pressing his forehead to mine. "You're my person. I hope you know that."

With a nod, I place the cigarette between his lips and spark it up. He takes a small drag before exhaling into the sky. A look of relief washes over him.

Draping my arm over his shoulder, I hold him close, and we walk down the street of Boston together in a blissful silence.

"What's up?" Micah questions, appearing unsure, making it evident that they're strangers.

"I'm sorry to interrupt," he begins. "I spotted you back at the entrance and just now finally got the guts to come introduce myself." He holds out his hand with a sheepish grin. "I'm Phil." They shake hands. "And you're hot."

"Oh," Micah replies. "Uh, thanks, Phil."

I shift on my heel, irritated. Stepping closer to Micah, I straighten my posture, my shoulders becoming tense. Rolling my eyes, I bring the rim of the glass to my lips.

"So, do *you* have a name?" Phil questions. "Or can I just call you mine?" I choke on my drink. "You want to dance?"

Micah grins. "Thanks, man, but I'm good right now. Maybe later."

"Okay, fine. So, what's it like being the most handsome guy in the room?"

"No," I grit out, throwing his arm around Micah's shoulder. "We're not doing this. Not tonight. Not ever."

"Don't be a dick, Jenny," Micah retorts, trying his best to keep the peace. He's acting like everything is fine and that's far from the truth. I know how bad he's hurting, and he's trying to fill the void with cheap beer and meaningless conversation. "Listen, I appreciate the compliments and all—"

Phil steps closer and attempts to kiss him. It happens so fast I almost miss it. Micah snaps his head to the side and pushes him back.

"Woah!"

Right away I grab this fucker by the throat and practically

lift him from the floor. "He's mine. Stay the fuck away from him," I warn, shoving him backward. Phil goes flying and then sprints away, escaping further into the crowd.

Several people around us stare.

Micah grabs his drink from the bar and chuckles.

"At least I have you to protect me from the occasional creeps," he easily replies, wiggling his eyebrows.

"Bathroom. Now."

"Huh?"

I grab him by the hem of his shirt and drag him through the crowd and toward the restrooms.

The second the bathroom door shuts behind us, the music cuts out slightly. The pounding beats and melodies still manage to seep through the walls, creating a subtle vibration beneath our feet. The harsh sting of the liquor lingers in the back of my throat as I swallow down the rest of my drink.

There are a few people in here, some standing by the mirrors that stretch from wall to wall, while the others engage in quiet conversations amongst themselves. The air is thick with cologne and sweat. Micah snatches his wrist from my hold and places his half empty glass on the counter by the sinks.

"What's your deal?" he asks. My body stiffens. "You get jealous back there?"

I grab his wrist and drag him toward the stalls, bumping my shoulder into someone along the way. "What the fuck, Jensen?" he growls, glancing behind us and giving the guy an apologetic stare. "My bad, man. He's crazy—"

I shove him inside the small cubicle and shut the door behind me, granting us a bit more privacy. He thinks this is a joke, shooting me a dazzling smile, except my steady gaze penetrates through me. His eyes bore into mine, his facial muscles turning tense and his eyebrows tightly furrowed.

"Stop drinking. Take it out on me instead."

When I lower my gaze, I take note of the large bulge in his jeans. "Well then," he lets out, readjusting his erection. "You really are jealous, aren't you?"

"Shut the fuck up," I snap. "Your cock. My mouth."

He releases a choked laugh. "Jesus Christ—"

"Now, Micah."

"How bad do you want it?" he tests, slowly pulling down the zipper as I drop to my knees.

"*Bad.*"

"Tell me," he encourages, admiring the eager look on my face as I stare up at him through my lashes. He's not the only one who feels betrayed and is seeking a distraction.

I waste no time slipping my fingers beneath the hem of his jeans, tugging on them with determination. He swats my hands away and clicks his tongue at me.

A low, feral groan escapes my chest. More anger arises. My cock jerks in response.

"No," he tells me. "I want to hear it."

I reach for him again, and this time he doesn't push me away. Slipping my hands beneath his shirt, I run my hands down his chest, my fingertips grazing along the contours of his toned abdomen. With a shudder, he moans softly. His body radiates warmth. I gaze up at him weakly, wanting nothing more than to feel his cock on my tongue.

I blink up at him, desperation flickering in my eyes. "I want it so fucking bad," I plead, faint whispers and amusement coming from outside the stalls. "Give it to me, Micah. Please."

With that, he pulls himself free. He works his thickness with his hand while I stare at the veins bulging with his movements, a small bead of precum leaking from the tip. "You're desperate for me." He lifts his shirt and pins it to his chest with his chin.

BLOODBATH

Staring at his cock, I nod, my mouth watering. "Yes," I groan.

"Show me."

I immediately take hold of him, twirling my tongue along the smooth head. His balls draw up. He's throbbing for me. While looking up at him and meeting his heated gaze, I suck the tip, our prolonged eye contact driving me wild. My dick twitches with need as he moves, thrusting his hips, my mouth gliding up and down nearly the full length. He inches forward and I take him fully, gagging as he passes the back of my throat. The saliva that has been building in my mouth drips down my chin and onto the floor.

"Holy fuck," he moans, drawing out each syllable.

He watches me closely, slamming his palms against both walls of the stall. His hands search for the top, his fingers curling around the thin edge. He buries his thick cock in the depths of my throat, choking me.

"Good boy," he whimpers. "Such a good fucking boy for me. Aren't you?"

"Mmm—"

"Don't talk with your mouth full."

I hum with fulfillment, increasing the suction and driving him to new heights. His breathing quickens in response.

"Get up," he commands, pulling me to my feet by my hair. I steal a long, passionate kiss from him before he spins me around and shoves me against the hard frame of the stall. "The need I have to bury my cock in your ass..."

"Do it."

"I don't have anything," he says desperately.

"Just spit in your hand," I instruct.

He tugs down his pants in a hurried frenzy, coating the head of his cock with saliva before pressing the tip into me. I push back against him, craving every inch.

"Easy," he mutters, pushing in slowly, but it's clear that isn't what either of us wants in this moment.

"Fuck me like you hate me, Micah."

Without wasting any time, he thrusts deeper, again and again. It's a tight fit, but fuck, I want this. He begins to slam into me savagely. God, he feels so much better than I remembered.

"Fuck," I choke out, my body tensing from pleasure and pain. "Oh my fucking—hell—"

Micah grips the back of my neck for leverage and grinds into me, his hips slapping against my ass with each thrust. As soon as he adjusts his angle, a gasp gets caught in the far back of my throat.

"Oh, fuck, *there*," I encourage, trembling. The urgent force behind his thrusts sends me forward, the side of my face thumping against the graffiti covered stall with each stroke. "Keep going. *Don't. Fucking. Stop.* Fuck, fuck, fuck."

"God, you feel amazing," he says through strained breaths.

Breathing hard, I stagger forward, my legs shaky. He rocks into me harder, fisting my hair, deepening his strokes.

"Look at you," he moans softly. "Bent over and taking my cock. Do you enjoy being my cum slut?"

"Yes."

"Louder."

Even with the door closed, it's clear we have an audience outside the stall. But I pay them no mind. The only thing I care about in this moment is giving Micah every part of me.

My heart. My soul.

My ass.

He curls his fingers around my throat without warning, taking away my ability to breathe. But then his grip loosens significantly. His body tenses. Breathing hitches. A soft whimper falls from his lips, and I know he's *there*.

"Give it to me," I beg loudly.

"Yeah?"

"I want every drop."

"Take my cum, baby," he groans, burying himself deeper.

Hunching forward, he spills himself inside me, but his thrusts don't stop. I reach behind me, digging my fingertips into his hip.

"*Micah*," I moan, my orgasm vibrating through my body.

My arms go limp as he begins to soften inside me. The second he pulls out, I stumble. He catches me just in time. He leans back against the solid frame of the stall, bringing me with him. There's so much passion in his eyes. For a moment I actually believe it's going to take me out.

Cupping his face with my hand, I lean closer, pressing my lips against his, savoring everything about him.

The way he tastes. The way he feels.

"First me, now you," he whispers into our kiss, tightly gripping my jaw. "Jealousy suits you better. You're so fucking hot."

He pulls me against his chest, tilting his head to the side and deepening our kiss, his tongue exploring my mouth hungrily. Sparks fly. My body quivers from his touch as he runs one hand through my hair, and the other down my back.

"Who needs meds when I have you?" He traces my lip with the tip of his tongue.

"Not funny."

"I think I'm hilarious."

Drawing back, I set my eyes on his.

"I love you," I breathe. "I fucking love you. Don't lie to me. Don't keep shit from me. Don't hide from me. Ever. Promise me."

He slams his mouth against mine, kissing me with a need to express these powerful emotions. When we part, our lips are swollen and red, faces flushed.

"Promise," he whispers back.

My heart thumps wildly. "If that fucker even glances in your direction again, I will carve out his eyes and make him eat them."

"Always so romantic. You should get jealous more often."

"Not so sure about that," I mutter, cleaning myself with toilet paper and then flushing it. "Now I'm going to have a funny limp when I walk for the rest of the night."

"You asked for it."

"I did," I confirm, watching him tuck his dick back into his pants.

We step out of the confined stall and walk past several people who can't seem to take their eyes off us. One girl literally grabs her boyfriend by the jaw to redirect his attention to her, as if they weren't just admiring the show together.

Fuck, I'm sore.

"Yup," I exhale sharply as we exit the bathroom. "I wasn't too far off."

Micah lowers his gaze to the screen of his phone, and I do the same.

> **Damien:** Taking Quinn to the penthouse. Meet us there.

Neither of us reply. Another text comes through.

> **Damien:** Please?

"At least he said please," I joke.
"Whatever. I hate him."

"No, you don't."

He glances at me with vulnerable eyes. "How would you know?"

I remain silent, wondering if he's ready for the answer. A huge part of me feels like this isn't the time or place to even be having this discussion, but another part of me has been curious.

"Well? I'm waiting."

"Maybe now isn't the best time."

He pulls me to a stop in the dimly lit hallway. "Just spit it out."

"You really want me to say it?"

"I do."

"I see the way you look at him," I reveal, stepping toward him and closing the space between us.

At first, a hint of panic crosses his face. Then fear. Confusion. Irritation. Downright denial. He shakes his head dismissively, uncomfortable with my accusation.

"What are you talking about?"

"You don't hate him. You actually have real feelings for him."

"Feelings?" he repeats, appalled. "Are you out of your damn mind?"

"Tell me I'm wrong then. Tell me you don't feel something deeper for him." Stepping closer, I press my pointer finger against his sternum with each word, as if to make a point. "Tell me your heart doesn't race whenever he steps into the room." His lips part. "Tell me you've never thought about *being* with him."

"I haven't," he mutters, hesitating briefly. "I don't have—"

I study him closely, capturing the exact moment the realization hits his eyes.

And it hits him hard.

"Did you really not realize it until now?" I ask.

He clenches his jaw, looking like a deer caught in headlights. "I... apparently not. I mean, yeah, maybe I've fantasized about him, but I do that with a lot of people."

"You can definitely be attracted to someone without having feelings for them," I agree, "but I don't think that's the case with you and Damien."

"No way," he dismisses.

I shrug.

"He's always just been my friend. One of my best friends," he stammers, trying to wrap his head around this. "How does that happen? How didn't I notice?"

"I think it happened gradually. I had my suspicions until a few months ago when I started catching this spark in your eye, but I'm no expert, clearly. I just recently started figuring my own shit out."

"Do you feel some type of way about it?" he questions, fidgeting with his hands.

"Do you?" I counter.

"I'm not sure. Are you seriously cool with this? Did I just make shit weird?"

Taking his hand, I shake my head. "I don't mind. I mean, I out of all people understand. It happened with us."

His lips curl into a subtle grin.

Holding up my hands, I shake my head. "I definitely don't have any romantic feelings for him, if that's what you're wondering," I say with a laugh. "We all have a bizarre thing going on. Damien and Quinn. Quinn and all of us. You and me."

"Good point."

"It works for us. All I know is I'm happy if you're happy."

"He's my friend," he says faintly. "I don't want to ruin that. Make it messy. He's not into me, anyway."

"I don't know. I've caught him checking you out a few times."

"When?"

"The bathroom the other night, for starters. When you had the towel wrapped around your waist."

"He was just goofing off."

"Whatever you say."

"All I want to do right now is kick him in the balls," he retorts, draping his arm around my waist as I head for the bar.

He pulls me in the direction of the door. "I'm good. I already got my fix."

"Oh, yeah? What's that?" I ask.

"*You.*"

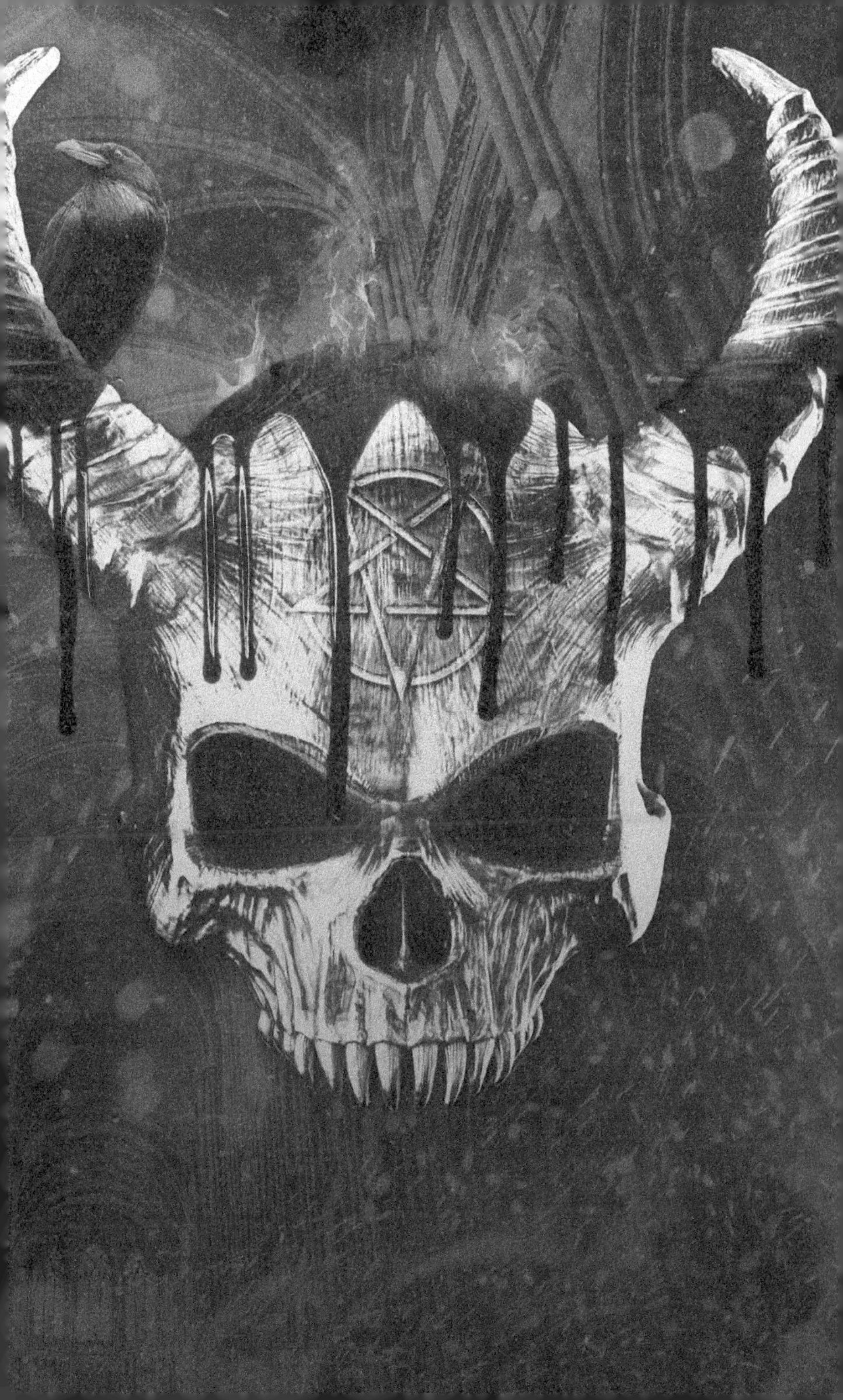

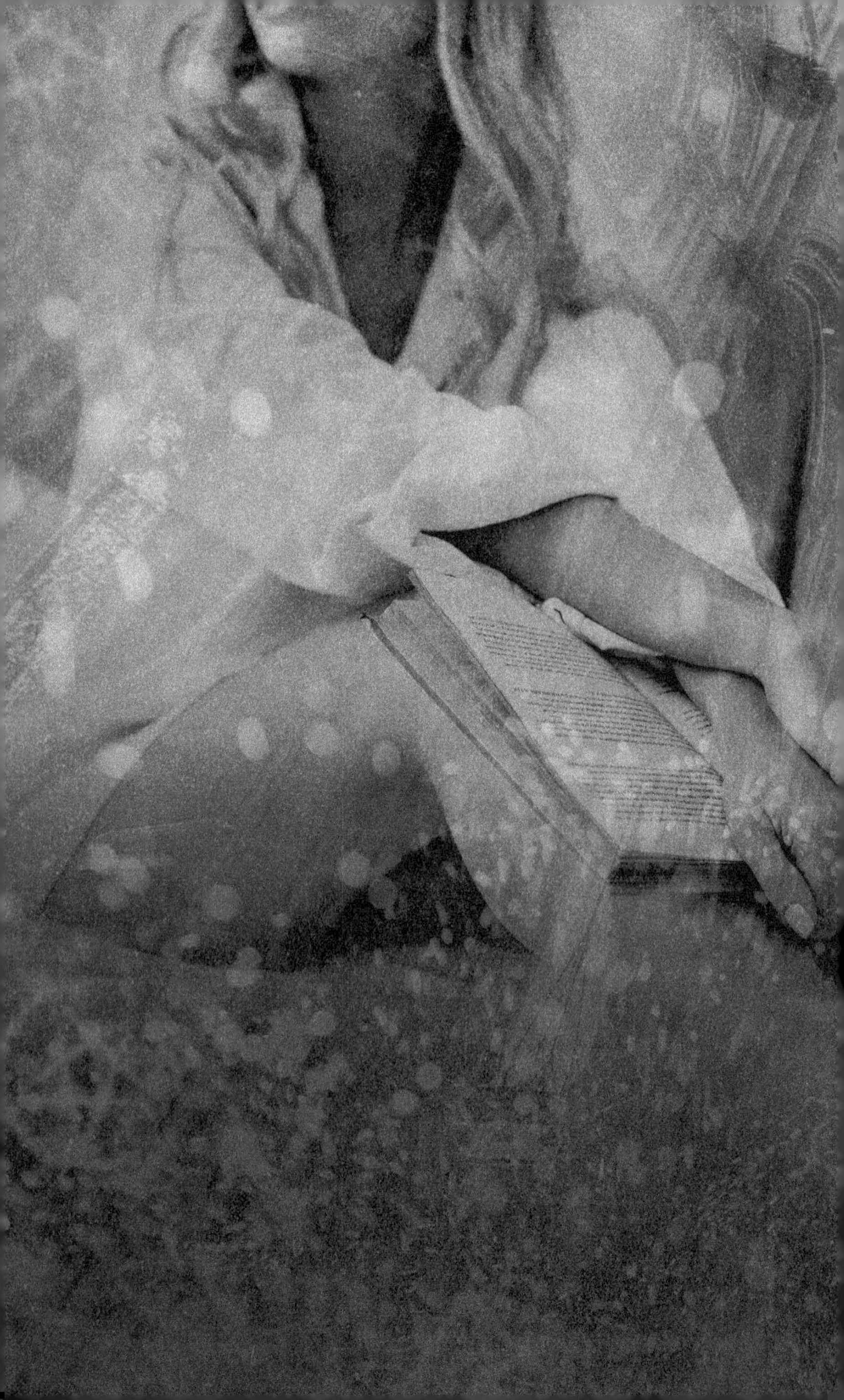

CHAPTER 16

QUINN

I'm immediately greeted by elegance and luxury, the interior design featuring floor to ceiling windows overlooking the cityscape of Boston, with high ceilings and an open layout. I've never been inside a luxury penthouse suite before.

With a cult after me, it makes sense he would bring me here.

"Is this place yours?"

He nods. "Ours," he clarifies. "What's mine is yours, and what's yours is yours."

The sun is rising, and the natural light and panoramic

views that surround us are almost overwhelming for me. I've never been this high up.

"My uncle left it to me after he died," he explains.

There's sleek designer furniture, mostly black in color, eliciting a seductive ambiance. When my attention meets the entrance to the terrace, Damien catches my apprehension. He presses his body into my back and embraces me.

"Not a fan of heights?" he asks, resting his chin on my shoulder.

With a nervous gulp, I shake my head. "I guess not."

"I'm sorry."

"It's fine. I've just never been this high up before."

"No," he breathes, turning me to face him. He cups my face with his hands and locks his eyes with mine. "*I'm sorry*, Quinn. I never meant to hurt you."

Tears spring to my eyes.

"I… I love you, Quinn, with every part of me." He takes my hand and places it over his chest. His heart beats steadily beneath my palm, reminding me that he's human. That sometimes people make mistakes.

"I didn't think I could feel this way. I didn't know I was capable of …loving… someone. You are my whole fucking world. I refuse to ever walk through life without you. I vowed to protect you. To keep you safe. But I failed you. I fucking failed you, Quinn. I'm so sorry I failed you. I'm so sorry I kept you in the dark. You didn't belong there. Especially not when you've only ever been my light."

"I'm not sure what to feel right now," I admit.

"It's okay. I'm here."

"Omen knew my mother," I say, a twinge of pain settling in my chest. "He told me she raised him. She had to have been a good person to give me a better life. Right?"

With a nod, he brings me closer.

"My whole life has been a lie," I whisper.

"Not this," he breathes softly, his forehead pressed to mine.

He leans down and presses a tender kiss on my lips. I can taste the saltiness from his tears coating my lips. This kiss is powerful, more meaningful than any other kiss we've shared in the past. This is binding.

Soul tying.

"I want to forgive you," I hum against his lips.

"I'm not worthy of your forgiveness. Not yet. But I swear on my life, I will do everything in my power to make it up to you." He draws back slightly, tracing my jaw with his fingertips. "I am going to slaughter them, Quinn," he promises, his face hardening, eyes darkening. "Every last one of them."

Damien links his fingers through mine and gives me a tour of the rest of the place. The thing I enjoy most is the privacy we have. Even perched above the busy city life below us, it's so quiet up here. Though he's made it clear that this penthouse was left to him, Jensen and Micah have their own designated rooms.

Once we enter the primary suite, I make myself comfortable on the king size bed, taking in this moment of complete tranquility. I'm exhausted. Mind, body, and soul. Before I can even make sense of it, Damien is hovering over me, pinning me to the plush bedding.

I stare up at him with a profound sense of security, admiring the way the sun's rays caress his face. The soft light that casts on him brings out every contour, accentuating his features. I take his face in my hands and trace beneath his eyes, his cheeks, then slowly graze my fingertips along his sharp, chiseled jawline.

The contrast between his dark long lashes and light blue eyes creates such a beautiful blend. The connection we have is unlike anything I've ever experienced. I let out a content sigh, lost in the depth of his tender gaze. It's impossible to put my feelings for him into words. The hard edges of his smirk begin to melt away and a moment of intimacy washes over us. His eyes soften, and he invites me in, connecting with me on a more heartfelt level.

A breath gets trapped in my chest as his gaze drifts to my mouth. Without wasting another second, our lips collide. Damien kisses me gently, like I'm the most precious gift in his world. My arms find their way around his neck and I bring him closer. He holds me so tight.

I've always felt so safe in his arms, and even after everything that has happened tonight, that hasn't changed.

"I refuse to ever let you go," he murmurs, pressing tender kisses along the curve of my throat.

Micah and Jensen appear in the doorway.

Damien frantically leaps off the bed and meets them across the room, a look of worry in his eyes. "I fucked up, and I owe you both an explanation—"

"Damn right you do," Jensen scoffs.

"But not now," Micah speaks over him. "I'm tired of being angry. I'm really, *really* tired."

"I'm sorry," Damien says, "and I know sorry isn't fucking good enough."

"You're right," Jensen replies. "It's not."

"There's a lot of bad blood between Omen and I. I thought if I acted like he didn't exist, then maybe he would fuck off forever. Disappear into the fucking abyss."

"Isn't that a bit harsh?" I ask from the bed. "He's still your brother."

"No, Quinn. He's not. Blood doesn't mean shit."

"Can we finish this later?" Micah questions.

Damien closes the space between them, placing a reassuring hand on Micah's shoulder. "If you want me to leave, I will. I'll leave, Micah. I'll give you time. As long as it takes."

Jensen and I lock eyes from across the room.

"Okay," Micah states.

Damien heads for the door, and the whole world begins to shatter.

"Wait—don't. That's the last thing I want," Micah clarifies with a sigh, grabbing his wrist and pulling him back to them. "We care about you, Damien. I don't want you to leave."

"None of us do," Jensen adds.

Damien's lips part. "Really?"

Micah caresses his arm. "I don't ever want that. I just want us all to be okay."

Damien grins. "You want me to stay?"

"I do. Come here."

The three of them embrace one another and set their eyes on mine.

"Get in on this, baby girl," Jensen calls to me.

"We're so sorry, babe," Micah coos.

Suddenly, I find myself joining where they stand. Micah and Jensen begin to apologize continuously, as remorseful and sincere as ever, offering no excuses. Them taking accountability means the world to me, but instead of responding with my words, I use my touch, starting with my lips, and the rest of my body follows.

Falling into their arms and breathing each of them in, one by one, then all at the same time. Because we are a team, and we're best when we're together.

"Move in with us, Quinn," Damien declares, his eyes locked with mine.

"Be with us, always," Jensen says.

Micah presses a gentle kiss on my temple.

"Okay." I pull them closer. "But only on one condition."

Damien nods.

Then Jensen and Micah join in.

DAMIEN

All three of us grab hold of our little Quinn, our hands and lips caressing her body. The sexual tension suddenly becomes too much to endure. I get caught up in the intense feelings of expressing our love and end up meeting Micah's eyes.

I've hurt him so much. It physically pains me.

And finally, I can't take the distance between us anymore. The emotional connection is there—maybe it always has been—and I don't want to resist for one more second.

Staring at his lips, I find myself leaning in, surveying his reaction to my proximity. His hand cradles the back of my head and brings me closer, giving me a few seconds to react, to push him away.

But I do the opposite.

"Fuck it," I mutter, slamming my mouth against his.

With soft brushes of the lips and synchronized movements, my heart pounds. As passion builds, a powerful feeling of warmth and solitude comes over me. This moment between us feels personal, like we're the only ones in the room.

Micah melts into me, our pulses quickening. The kiss deepens and tensions grow high, our breathing shallow and urgent, but a blissful silence stretches through my mind, even with exploring this new territory for the first time.

Kissing Micah feels good.

Quinn and Jensen join in on this spontaneous display of

affection, their lips and tongues entwined with ours. Even without saying a word, there's a mutual understanding between the four of us. We all care for each other... hell, we would do *anything* for each other.

It's never been about *parts* to me. It's about the connection.

They're teaching me that it's okay to be *me*, that it's okay to allow myself to love the people I love.

They're teaching me to love and accept *myself*.

Because this is who the fuck I am.

And no matter what I've been trained to believe by my father... I'm enough.

We all strip each other, kissing and groping one another, leaving a trail of discarded clothing on the floor. Quinn moves me toward the bed and I fall backward, staring up at her in awe.

She looks like a fucking angel. I stroke my cock from tip to base, my thumb grazing over the cuts, while Micah and Jensen fall on the bed beside us.

Quinn straddles my waist. My cock twitches as she grazes the pad of her thumb over the smooth, rosy slit, wiping away the evidence of my arousal. The muscles in my pelvic region contract, my back briefly arching from the mattress.

"Fuck," I bite out, my biceps flexing as I rest my arms above my head, watching as Micah takes Jensen's cock into his mouth.

Quinn's thighs are already drenched as they hug my hips. She lightly grazes her pussy along the length of my shaft, sliding back and forth, the friction of it sending a spark through me. I eagerly buck my hips upward. My quiet groans are her encouragement.

Her full breasts bounce as she leans forward, taking hold of my wrists and securing them in place beside my head. I swallow hard, staring up at her with dilated pupils and slightly swollen lips. My dick twitches, smacking against her clit. I groan, sucking my bottom lip into my mouth and taking in the sight of her beautiful skin and puckered nipples.

She tightens her hold on my wrists and grinds her slick pussy against my dick, a hushed moan falling from her lips. "Do you want to switch?" she asks me.

I nod. "Switch with Micah."

With a satisfied grin, she climbs off me, and Micah's eyes set on mine.

"What?" he asks, his voice hoarse.

I reach for his hand, and when I find it, I bring it to my lips, sucking his fingers into my mouth.

"Fuck, Damien," he breathes sharply.

"Come here."

Quinn and Micah switch places, and I remain on my back. A gasp falls from Jensen's lips as he slips inside our beautiful girl. Micah takes my pulsating cock in his hand while gauging my reaction. Adrenaline surges through my body. I can see him more clearly than ever.

He strokes me from tip to base, working slowly at first, a hint of uncertainty flickering in his eyes until I begin bucking my hips. The moment he leans down and traces the veins of my shaft with his tongue, I inhale a sharp breath, my chest rising and falling, hard and fast.

"Fuck," I curse, watching with intense anticipation as he twirls his tongue around the tip. "Oh, fuck." The sensation of his warm, plump lips sends me to heights I didn't even know existed.

"Mmm," Micah moans, gliding his tongue along the full length of my dick before focusing on the initials of our beautiful girl.

He spells out both letters with the tip of his tongue, and I savor the sting, my balls tightening. As sensitive as it is, I'm a sucker for the pain.

Fuck, I crave it.

He takes me into his mouth, sucking and licking, bobbing his head up and down. I'm swept up in the feeling of how tight his throat is, so I grab the back of his head and push myself further, holding him in place.

"Fucking Christ. Fuck. Micah."

He chokes, and gags, spit coating my cock as he draws back, desperate for air. With flushed cheeks and watery eyes, he looks at me—*really* looks at me.

Suddenly we see each other in a whole new light.

I guide him back down, fucking his face with urgent thrusts, hitting the back of his throat harder and harder, groaning loudly over the sound of his muffled whimpers.

"Fuck, if you don't stop, I'm going to come," I warn.

He doesn't listen.

Hell, maybe he does, but just doesn't care.

Because Micah continues giving me some of the best head of my life, bringing me closer to the edge with each second that passes.

Time falls away. I can almost hear the wet sounds of his mouth over the echoing sounds of Jensen's balls smacking against Quinn's thighs as he takes her from behind. She's watching us eagerly with flushed cheeks and a seductive smile.

Right before I'm about to explode, I fist his hair, yanking him off me. He's gasping for air at this point, his lips red and swollen, the corners of his mouth raw.

"Fuck me, Damien, please," he begs. Pushing him onto all fours, I climb behind him, trying to catch my breath. "Are you good?" he asks breathlessly.

"Fuck yeah, I am," I groan, fisting my dick tight. "Are you?"

"I'll be better once I have your cock inside me. Let me feel you."

I oblige, spitting into my palm and coating his back hole with saliva. He glances back at me with heated eyes as I sink two fingers into his ass. He's tight as fuck. My dick grows harder as I press the head of my cock against his ass and thrust into him slowly.

"Holy— fuck," he chokes out, his body tensing.

He cries out euphorically with each inch. Soon enough, I give him the entire thing. I lean my front against his back, my forehead resting on his shoulder as I enter him deeper.

He's the only man I've ever been inside of, and it feels so fucking amazing. I drill him into the bed, sinking into his tight hole, cursing out profanities, our bodies slick with sweat.

"Oh—my fucking—" Micah calls out loudly, reaching behind him and digging his fingertips into my hip. "Oh hell, *Damien, please*—"

Breathing out harshly with each stroke, and my pelvis smacking against his ass, I enter him harder, my balls clapping against his thighs.

"Take him deeper, Micah," Jensen praises from beside us while pounding into Quinn. "Good fucking boy."

"Don't tell him that," I groan, tightening my grip on his waist and driving into him with more force.

He whimpers, his palm flat against the headboard.

"He's doing so fucking good," Quinn moans softly, rolling her hips and grinding against Jensen's pelvis.

"He's nothing but a greedy slut, begging for my dick like a bitch," I degrade, leaking pre-cum inside him.

"Look at how bad he wants it," Jensen taunts.

"Are you going to come for me, Micah?" I breathe beside his ear. "Are you going to come for me while my thick cock is buried deep in your ass?"

"Fuuuck—yes," Micah cries, sliding back and forth on my length.

"Give it to me," I demand, his warm walls spasming around me as I rock into him.

It doesn't take long before his body tenses beneath mine. It happens fast. He smothers his face into the pillow and screams, coming intensely.

Quinn's moans echo against the walls, her legs wrapped around Jensen as she approaches her climax. She reaches out for me, and I take her hand, interlocking my fingers with hers. Jensen's fingers dig into her skin as he throws his head back and shuts his eyes.

All it takes is five more thrusts and I explode into one of the strongest orgasms I have ever had. Yeah, I've done anal before, but with Micah, it's different.

It's a new favorite of mine that I'll continue to indulge in.

The four of us all find our release at the same time—me burying myself deep and spilling myself inside Micah, Quinn coming with a cry, and Jensen groaning as he collapses on top of her.

We're all drained of both energy and cum. It's been a long, torturous night, and the only thing getting me by is that I have them with me.

After several minutes pass and we finally catch our breath, I pull all three of them closer.

Quinn breaks the silence. "My condition, before I move in with you..." she begins, with serious eyes, and her chest rising and falling steadily with each breath. "I'm done with hiding, done with following your lead, and I am done being a victim." Suddenly, there's a spark in her eye, a spark that radiates strength, courage, and power. "I'm joining the Order."

I want to put my foot down and tell her fuck no. That it's dangerous. That joining the Order entails a dark fate that she cannot even imagine. That her initiation night alone could impact her in ways she never thought possible.

But there's this look in her eye that speaks to me on a level so profound, I feel like I'm staring into a mirror. She needs this.

The three of us exchange stares.

Micah, Jensen, and I.

They look scared.

Deep down, we know this is something we could never deny her, no matter how badly we want to. *Especially not now.*

The naïve little Quinn we once knew is no longer here.

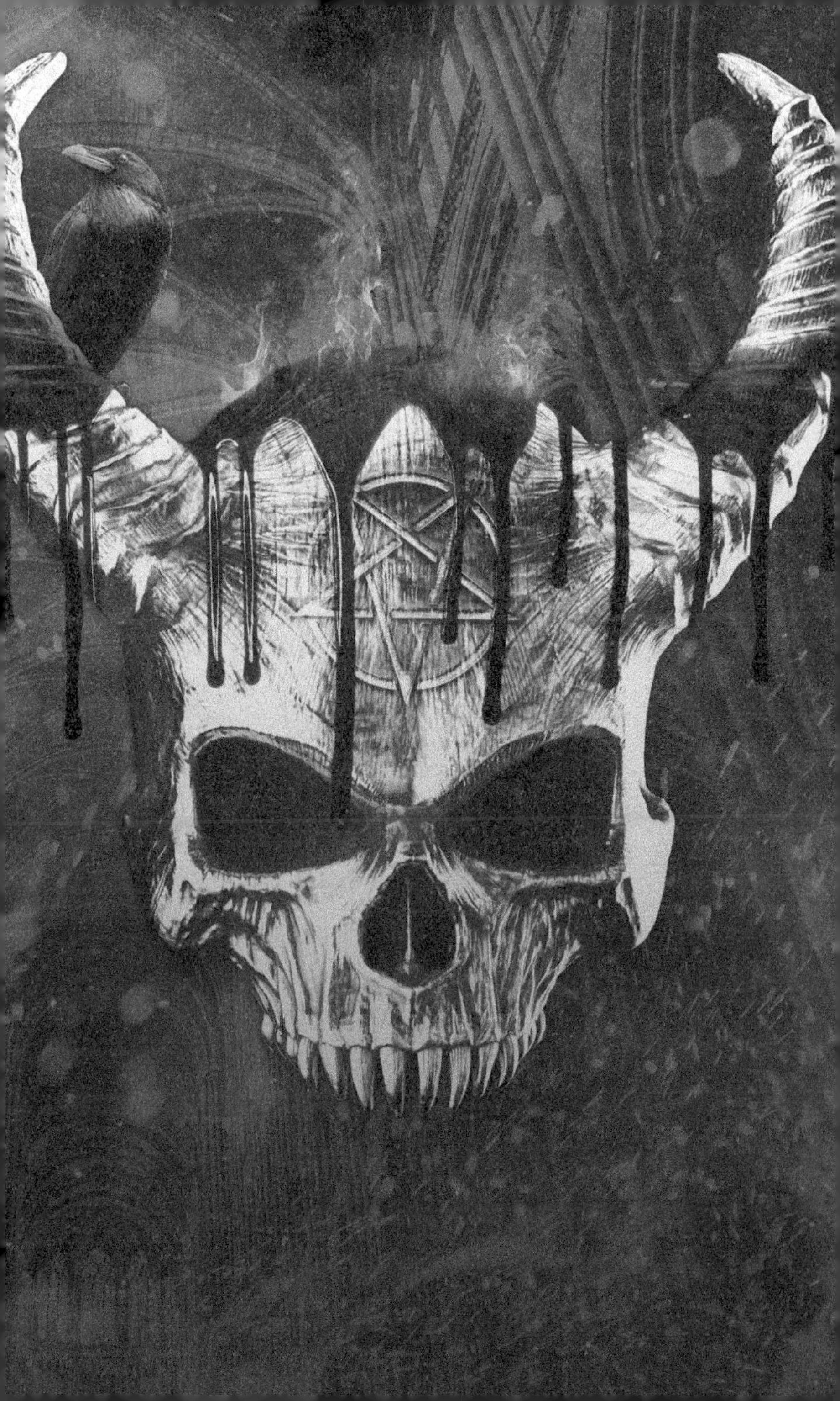

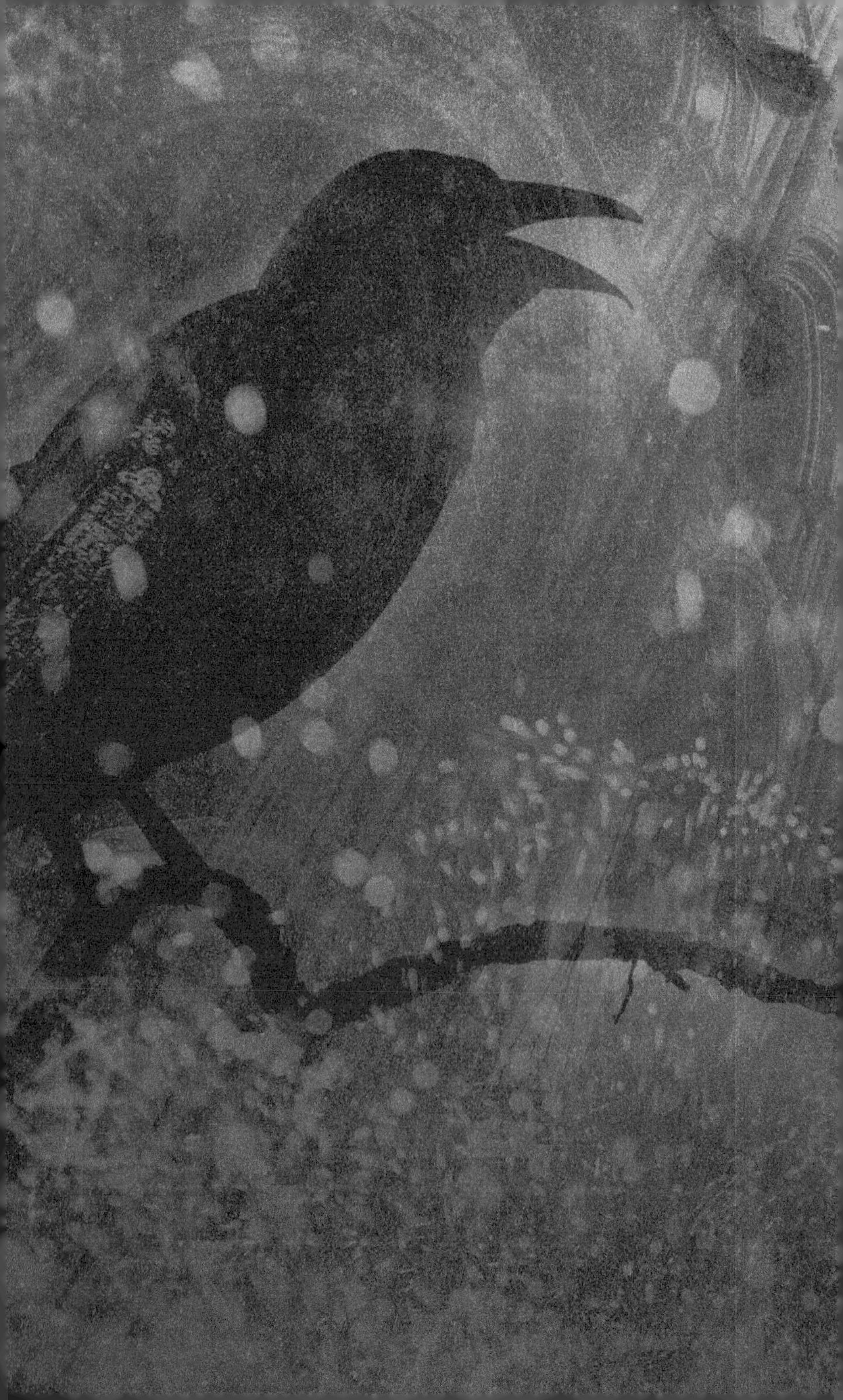

EPILOGUE

Unknown: Was so great finally seeing you, little bro

Damien: Two minutes and forty three seconds

Omen: And?

Damien: Cut the shit, Omen. What do you really want?

Omen: That's the thanks I get for doing your dirty work?

Damien: Don't act like you did me a favor

Omen: Funny how you think I did it for you

Damien: If this is the part where you tell me you did it for her, I'll slit your throat

Omen: Stop you're scaring me

Damien: Daddy not giving you enough attention lately?

Omen: Now you're projecting. We both know you're the one with daddy issues

Damien: Yet he trained you to be his bitch

Omen: Didn't Quinn tell you? I've gone rogue. Daddy keeps trying to tell me what to do, but I'm nobody's puppet. I'm the one pulling the strings

Damien: Then leave

Omen: I will. But not until he's ten feet under. You can trust me

Damien: Why the fuck would I do that

Omen: Because we can help each other

Damien: I don't need your help

Omen: You don't know what's coming. But I do. I know everything

Damien: Prove it then. Bring one of them to me. Show me where your true loyalty lies

Omen: Drop a location. I'll deliver him hand wrapped with a pretty pink bow around his neck

Damien: Harmony Grove Cemetery. Tonight. 11 PM.

Omen: You mean the one near your not-so-safe house? Why don't I save you the trouble and bring him straight to you? I won't charge extra for express delivery. Pinky swear

Damien: We'll be waiting

Omen: That's it? You're no fun. Tell me all the filthy things you're gonna do to him

Damien: If you fuck us over... Nothing compares to what I'm going to do to you

Omen: I'm shaking. But not from fear. Is now the appropriate time for me to send you a dick pic? See u tonight <3

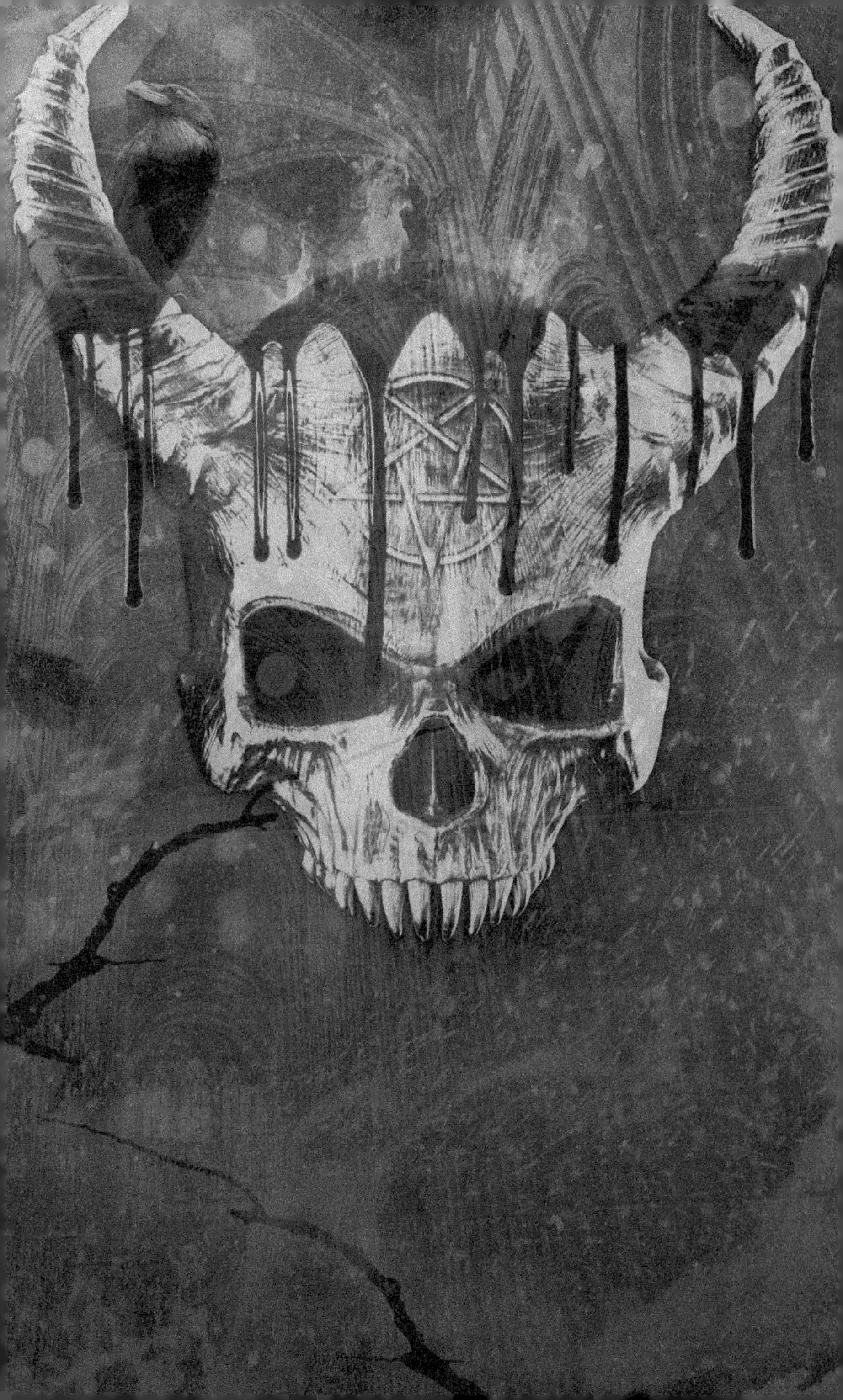

ACKNOWLEDGEMENTS

Havoc, Harper, Kylie, & Leah
You are the best team anyone could ever ask for. Thank you for all your hard work and dedication. Honestly have no idea what I would do without you. You support and love me in more ways than you know and I love my Chaos Crew to the moon and back

Charly
I can't even find the words. You do so much for me, always going above and beyond, and as annoying as I am… you still tolerate me. You're such a talented artist and the cover/formatting for this book is so sexy I'm unable to stop crying and screaming

Santana
You quite literally saved my ass and now I owe you my soul. Seriously though, you're an incredible friend

Genesis, Em, Macie, Brittany
I asked for what I thought was impossible, but yall delivered. As always!!! I appreciate you so much and thank you for all your help, ideas, and encouragement along the way. Can we never talk about the dumpster fire of the first draft?

Hanna, Caitlin, Taylor
Thank you for your time, feedback and patience. It's important to me as an author to make sure I'm educated and that my readers can relate to my characters and their experiences. Damien also wanted me to mention he appreciates the three of you for your guidance

Jessica
My sister, my bitch, my shoulder to cry on
Thank you for being my best friend/sister/pain in the ass for the past 15 years. Damn, we're old. I'm still waiting for you to publish your first book, so can you hurry the fuck up? I love you

To my readers, ARC & Street team
I never know what to say here because words will never be enough

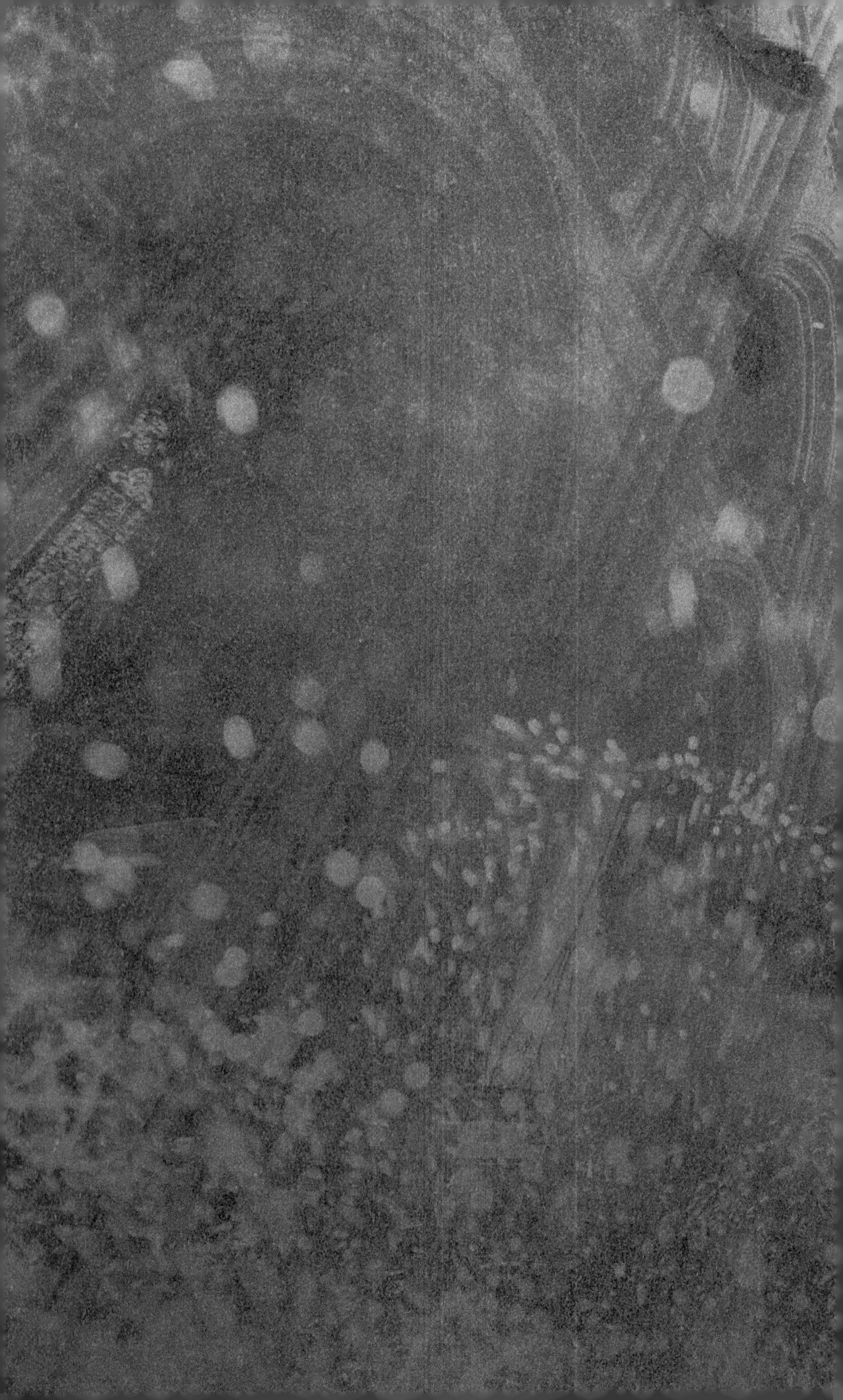

ABOUT THE AUTHOR

Molly Doyle has been writing since she was in grade school, and has been a published author since she was sixteen. Once she moved her talents to an online platform, her writing took off. She has reached millions of readers across the globe, with many of them crediting her for their mask kink. When she's not fantasizing about masked men, she's plotting her next erotic story.

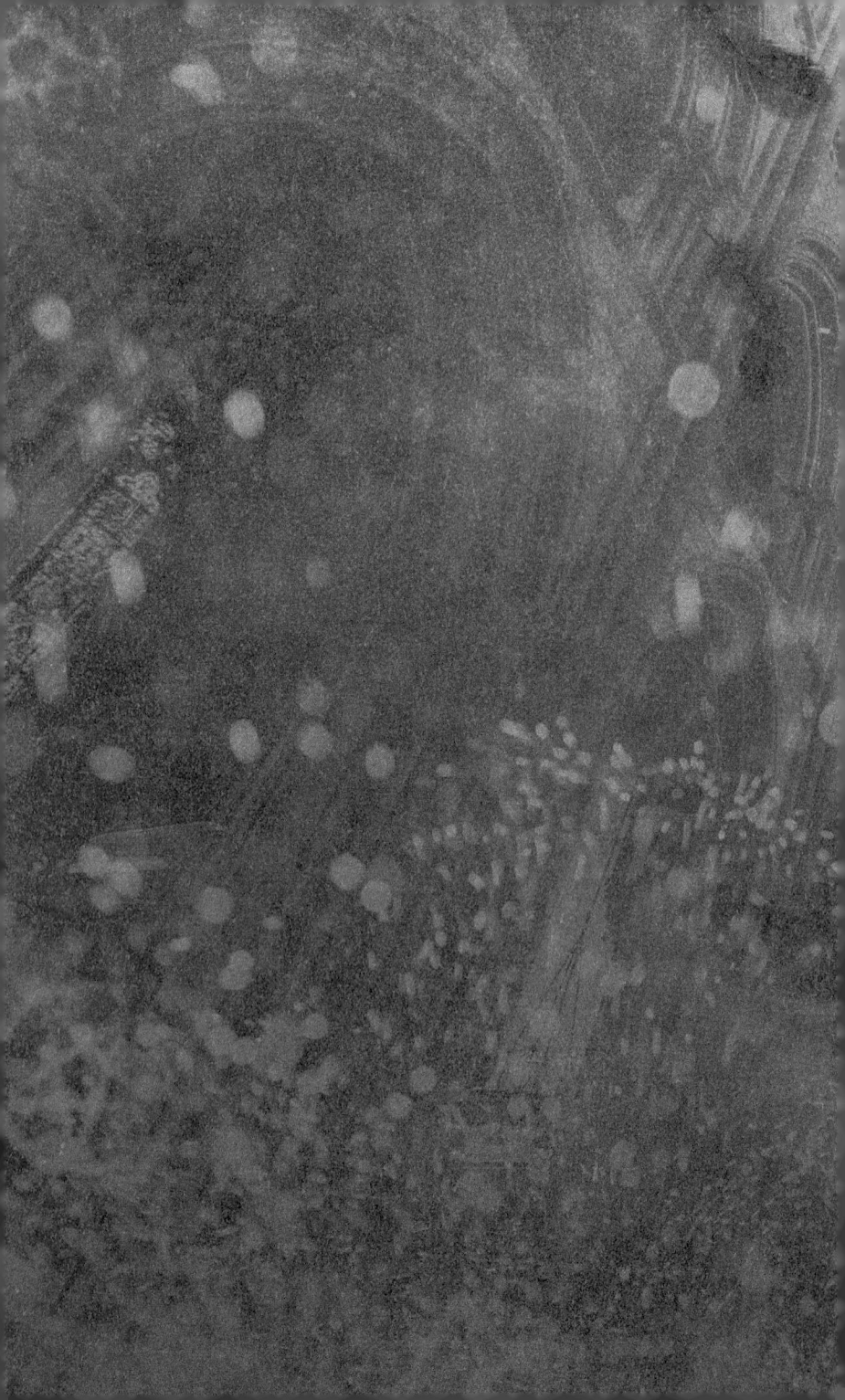

ALSO BY MOLLY DOYLE

DESIRES DUET
DOMINANT DESIRES
DARK DESIRES

ORDER OF THE UNSEEN
SCREAM FOR US
BLOODSHED
MELT FOR US
BLOODBATH
TBA

Milton Keynes UK
Ingram Content Group UK Ltd.
UKHW031303251024
450245UK00004B/303